ENVISION

FUTURE FICTION

Print Edition
ISBN 978-1-927830-16-1

I0598499

Kathy Steinemann

Contributing Authors
John Bryant, Michael Donoghue, M. K. French,
Laura Alexandra Hunter, Rubin Johnson,
Kip McKnight, Michael Siciliano, Luke Walters

Foreword by Katie Stephens

Human-Created

Dedicated
to the writers and readers
at Scribophile.

Thanks
to Katie Stephens
for writing the foreword

and to all the contributing authors:

John Bryant
Michael Donoghue
M. K. French
Laura Alexandra Hunter
Rubin Johnson
Kip McKnight
Michael Siciliano
Luke Walters

TABLE OF CONTENTS

Foreword 1

Artifice..3
The Ministry of Procreation...................................22
Serve and Protect..26
Salvation..37
The Persistence of Silica..43
Evolution..47
Unknown Scyphozoa 58
Settlement Standards 63
What Comes After...66
Alien Irony..74
Artless...77
Unwired 88
The Demise of Great Expectations 95
Easy As 100
You Bet Your Life 104
Home...112
Memory Card 116
The Perils of Traveling Interplanetary Pod Class....119
Minus 124
Newton's Second Law 128
Quid Pro Quo..130
Sanitation Protocols..134
Window Washers..135
Square-Fare...144
Still Here 147
Competing for Kallista 151
Fluxxatron Malfunction 163

Afterword 173

About the Editor 174

Books by Kathy Steinemann 175

FOREWORD

Katie Stephens

What can the future bring? My favorite authors, from Robert Heinlein to Andre Norton and Jules Verne to JD Robb, use scientific models to dream and develop their stories, bringing their readers into worlds that years later often come true. Every time I read a story in the science fiction genre, I wonder if the concept propagates because someone has the scientific knowledge to develop the particular idea, or if prophets live amongst us and deign to write science fiction. I am constantly astonished at the complex world building and workings of the minds that bring this genre to life.

In *Envision,* Kathy Steinemann presents a number of up-and-coming sci-fi authors, mostly members of the Scribophile community. She has discovered an excellent blend of stories from writers published for the first time as well as authors who can add this book to their bios and résumés. Kathy also includes a few of her own amazing stories — an added bonus!

In these works, the reader shall encounter robots that may or may not be alive, future space travel that doesn't seem so different than what we encounter today — but with a twist, knowledge of the afterlife, and the perils of procreation, as well as many other adventures.

Close the curtains, light a lamp, and cozy up with a hot cup of tea, chocolate, or coffee. You won't be able to put this book down.

-—-•••••-—-

IF YOU DISCOVERED a sealed box with "Katie's memories" scribbled on the side, you'd find a lifetime of partially completed stories, plays, and musicals. A retired music teacher, **Katie Stephens** has opened that box and writes both non-fiction and fiction, where she happily experiments with all genres. Her adult literature has been published in *Spark: A*

Creative Anthology, The Bella Online Literary Review, and on Kathy Steinemann's website (a little horror flash titled "Baby Talk"). Her latest romance release is in the anthology *Propose To Me,* where she delves into the realm of witchcraft.

Katie's alter ego, K.T. Stephens, writes YA and children's books, and is especially enamored of the circus. Just mention acrobats and strongmen, and she'll jump headfirst into this world of magic, color, and precision and take you with her! You can find her young adult stories in the first two volumes of *Seven Deadly Sins, A YA Anthology,* where she is both an author and co-editor.

When her muse takes a break, Katie is a staff reader for *freeze frame fiction* and a grant writer for the Empire & Great Jones Creative Arts Foundation. Although her grown children are scattered east and west across the country, she lives solidly in mid-America with two kitties and a husband who keeps asking when she's really going to retire.

Follow Katie at standardishue.com.

ARTIFICE

-—-•◊•-—-

Kathy Steinemann

A SMALL GROUP of students at the 2020 Norse Archaeological Conference craned their necks as Professor Goodmann reached into a charred Norse cooking pot. "Ladies and gentlemen, are you ready for a mystery?" With a flourish, he pulled out an object and raised his gloved hand. Students strained to get closer to the weather-beaten iPhone with its broken touchscreen.

The professor lowered his voice. "You all look puzzled. You'll be even more puzzled when you learn that organic materials lodged within the cellphone are from the same century as this pot in which the phone was found."

Jaws dropped. Cameras clicked. Flashes flared.

"The phone is badly damaged, and the passage of centuries has caused so much corrosion that we've been unable to retrieve any identifying information. But we *were* able to restore a large portion of a fascinating photo: this Viking cooking pot in pristine condition. You can see a copy of the photo on the HD screen to your right. Note the distinctive groove in the lip that matches the indentation on this artifact."

The room erupted with gasps and buzzing conversation.

◊

Goodmann's biggest sceptic was his colleague, Professor Betruger — a tall, skinny malcontent with dark eyes and a large mole in the middle of his forehead. Betruger voiced his concerns on the early evening news. *"Goodmann is a fraud and a liar. He's devised a way to skew the radiocarbon dating process."*

◊

Theora Hafner hummed as she worked on reproductions for her Bidders-n-Bytes auction account. Her peanut-brown hair and the remnants of her 35th-birthday cake reflected some of the burbling brilliance from an antique lava lamp perched on the edge of the desk.

There.

The Viking thumb ring was perfect — shiny and almost as good as new. She sighed.

Too bad it's a fake.

◊

Eight blocks away, Erik Hammersson flicked a strand of blond hair off his laptop and held an index finger over the keyboard, ready to raise his bid if necessary.

No need.

The ring was his.

He arranged for payment. Then, he interlaced his fingers behind his neck. He stretched, gaze straying to the wall filled with shelf after shelf of Norse artifacts. Now he would have a warrior thumb ring.

Occasionally he managed to find authentic articles among the objects he bought online. Those he added to his collection. The remainder were stowed in a storage closet, destined to become flea-market merchandise someday.

He sighed and covered his face with his hands.

His eyes were moist when he adjusted the armrests of his chair and refocused his concentration on the computer.

◊

A few days later, the package containing Erik's purchase arrived. He sliced through generous layers of transparent tape and removed the bubble wrap.

He trembled. His heart pumped faster, and his eyes flashed with excitement as he forced the ring onto his thumb.

◊

Theora enjoyed Saturday mornings at the local flea market — always new treasures and interesting people. Near the quilting display, she bumped into a broad-shouldered man with blond hair and an engaging smile.

He bowed. It was a slight movement. Almost imperceptible. "Good morning, Miss ..."

Her pulse leaped. His voice with its slight accent made her shiver. She tried to imitate his bow. "Hafner. Theora Hafner."

He wasn't tall, but his presence was commanding. "Erik Hammersson. Pleased to meet you. Bargain hunting?"

She moistened her lips. "Um, I buy things and resell them online. I also create pottery reproductions. Couldn't find a job I liked in my field of expertise, so I reinvented myself."

"Your field?"

"I have a PhD in Modern Languages, but what I needed was a J.O.B., so here I am: auction queen by day, potter by night." She rubbed her upper lip. *That accent. German maybe? Or Icelandic? It's certainly not a Romance language.*

He swayed, arms crossed, appraising her. "I've seen your profile on Bidders-n-Bytes. You sold me this." He extended his thumb.

Theora's jaw dropped. "I ..."

Erik's cheeks dimpled. "You look surprised."

"I was very clear in the description that it's only a reproduction, and you got it for a great price." She glared. "So what's your complaint, Mr. Hammersson?"

His response came out as a whisper. "It's real, not a reproduction." When Theora's mouth flew open, he withdrew a pace. "If you're not careful you'll trap a fly in there."

"But how could you — I mean — It's real?"

His smooth voice coaxed a quiver in her shoulders. "Would you mind coming to my place? I can show you why I bought the ring."

"You expect me to follow a strange guy to who-knows-where for who-knows-what?"

"You can ask a friend to come along."

"No need," she said as she sized him up and felt for the pepper spray in her purse.

His face brightened with a grin. "Pepper? Or mace?"

She brushed him away. *Cocky son of a B.*

He escorted her down the block. She followed, lips pursed, and snapped a photo of his license plate.

Erik opened the passenger door of his white Mustang. "I don't usually ask strange women to accompany me in my chariot."

"Nothing strange about me." She tossed her hair, and ignored the door.

With a chuckle, he continued to hold it for her. The chuckle was a throaty sound. Safe. Comfortable. Reassuring.

She glanced his way. "What's your address? I'm texting a friend to tell her where we're going. And hold still while I take your picture. She'll get that along with a photo of your license plate."

"You don't take chances. Good." He handed her a business card.

She snatched it from him. "And I'll take my own car, thank you very much!"

◊

Erik led her to a neighborhood near the university, and parked next to a small condo. She followed him up the sidewalk but stopped at the entrance. His blue eyes twinkled with the innocence of Santa Claus. "I'll leave the door open. Don't worry, I won't try anything."

"Just so you're aware, I have a black belt in Taekwondo." She transferred her pepper spray into a pocket, propped her purse against the door, and scrutinized the Viking relics in the living room. They appeared authentic. She admired the pieces and stroked them with her fingertips while Erik watched and waited.

Her voice wavered. "The ring is real?"

"Yes. See this gash in the metal?"

She moved closer. *He smells good. Reminds me of fresh air and red licorice.*

"The gash happened when I ... I know it's real because I saw it catalogued in an online collection."

"Who *are* you?"

"I'm ... I'm sorry. I never should have said — Could you please tell me where you got it?"

"I discovered it in a cave last month when I was hiking."

He paced. "I must find that cave."

"Why?"

"I'm not sure I can explain. Would you help me? Please?" His expression made him look like a lost little boy.

She bit her lower lip. "I'm not sure I could locate it again. It's off the trail, and everything looks the same out there."

"Would you try?"

"I guess so."

Even though she assured herself everything would be all right, she felt a tiny sliver of worry creep to her brow.

◊

As soon as Theora returned home, she scoured the internet for information about Erik. He was well-respected, with a consultant's position at the museum. Several of his articles about Norse culture had been published in literary journals, and he was a keynote speaker at an upcoming archeological conference in San Francisco.

She closed her laptop and called her girlfriend Anne. "I've checked him out, and he seems to be on the up and up."

"Yeah, I know who he is. He's kinda quiet though. Not my type. One of the girls in the office went out with him for a while."

Theora frowned. "Why did they break up?"

"She said he was into Viking legends and stuff. He spent too much time talking about that and not paying any attention to her. But he was a real gentleman. TOO much of a gentleman, if you get my drift."

"I hardly know him. Met him at the flea market. But there's something about the guy. Intriguing. Mysterious. And he's pretty easy to look at."

"Easy to look at? Girl, he's hot! If there's chemistry, go for it. Remember what I keep telling you."

"Yeah. Get out more."

◊

Theora's tongue wasn't active, but her thoughts were. *What in blazes am I doing out in the woods with a stranger? This isn't the smartest thing I've ever done.*

A Sunday afternoon breeze cooled their faces as they pushed through branches on the hillside. The sweet fragrance of wild roses helped to compensate for the thorny scratches inflicted on exposed skin. The pace kept them both winded.

Their conversation was polite. Safe. Impersonal. They searched until late afternoon, but decided to halt their hunt before it got dark.

When they neared the exit to the parking lot, Erik touched Theora's elbow. "Could we try again tomorrow? It's a long weekend, and I can take Tuesday off as well if need be. My hours are flexible."

A fleeting frown creased her forehead. "All right. I can juggle my auction activities too."

His head tipped slightly as though he were sizing her up. "Until tomorrow then?"

"Tomorrow."

They headed out shortly before twelve and shared a picnic lunch in a mossy clearing. Theora remembered the area. To the right stood an old, Y-shaped birch that looked as though lightening had stabbed it in the heart. To the left, a large rock with sparkles of iron pyrite.

The way Erik sat — with a confident smile, one knee bent, resting on an elbow while he chewed on a licorice twist — well, Theora's thoughts strayed far from Norse artifacts and Viking thumb rings.

He cleared his throat. "Anyone home in there? Are you ready to go now?"

She blinked. "Sorry, my mind was elsewhere. Sure. Anytime you are."

They located the cave early in the afternoon. She inhaled the familiar scent of mint and moss near the entrance as she peered through the darkness. "I didn't go in very deep. Why would anyone leave a valuable artifact *here*?"

"Someone stole it from me."

Theora retreated a step. "You said it's authentic. That it belongs to you." She chuckled. "Are you telling me you're hundreds of years old?"

"Hardly. I'm thirty-six. And you?"

"Didn't anyone ever tell you nice guys never ask a woman her age or weight?"

He winked. "I never claimed to be nice."

Maybe he's not so stodgy after all. She tried to sound gruff. "What in blazes is going on here?"

"I can't ..."

She inched forward. "You can trust me. How bad could it be?"

"Well ..." He stroked his beard for several seconds. "I've never told anybody this, but I guess you should hear my story before we go on. I'll give you a condensed version."

Theora leaned against a tree and listened, wide-eyed, while Erik spoke.

"At sixteen years of age, I found myself in a dark alleyway, wandering without memory or money. My clothing was different from the rags worn by the homeless people who slept on the street. I tried to converse, but everyone gawked at me as though I were a lunatic. Whatever had happened to me muddled my brain, and to make matters worse, I didn't understand a word of English. I stumbled about the inner city until the police picked me up."

Erik continued, squinting, as though trying to gauge her reactions. "The authorities processed me through the child-welfare system. I was lucky. Unlike many wards of society, I was taken in by loving foster parents who paid for my education. I graduated from high school and continued my studies, until I earned a PhD in Archaeology."

He steepled his fingers. "Fragments of memory resurfaced whenever I examined a Norse artifact. My unease grew, until finally I was certain something had transported me to a different century and location. I regained most of my memory, but I didn't tell anyone. Who would believe my story? Everyone would think I was delusional. So I've kept this a secret. Until now."

Theora scrutinized his face. Then she stared behind him, unfocused, into the blackness they were about to explore.

He grimaced. "You think I'm a lunatic, just like those people twenty years ago. I shouldn't have told you."

With his slouched shoulders and drooping blond head, Erik reminded Theora of a wilting sunflower she had once seen during a drought. A sad sigh escaped her lips. "I want to believe you."

Erik flinched. "I thought — I'm not sure what I thought. Let's keep going. If you still want to?"

Was he telling the truth? His story was so outlandish it *had* to be true. Did she trust him?

She nodded and took the lead.

They ducked under a large protrusion and stepped past three triangular stones that leaned together, forming a crude tripod. Their flashlights lanced through the darkness, flickering over boulders and dirt.

Theora stopped. "This is as far as I went. It's where I discovered your ring and turned back toward the trail. Let's go a few more yards." They stepped around a rock and —

Brilliant sunshine engulfed them as they almost walked off the edge of a cliff. Erik extended his arm to grab Theora, and they peered behind them.

The cave had disappeared. A pair of large rocks stood — petrified guards — marking the spot where they had come through. They retraced their steps and stood between the rocks. Then they rematerialized in the cave.

Erik shone his flashlight into Theora's face. "Do you believe me now?"

She retched.

He smoothed his fingers over her shoulders. "I forgot that part. When I came to in the alleyway twenty years ago, I puked my guts out."

Her reaction was a long moan. Then she spoke. "You're THOR-y?"

"You're well enough to tell Norse jokes? How about this groaner? Vali realized that his wife, Helga, had fallen out of the boat. It was quite a relief to him because an hour earlier, he figured he was going deaf."

She moaned again. "Are you saying I talk too much?"

"Only when you're nervous. Guess I do too, but ..." His grinning blush was visible even in the dim light. "So, how's your stomach?"

"Still not great, but it's improving." She leaned back against him, inhaled a huge breath, and released it. "I believe you now. Why aren't *you* nauseated?"

"Maybe it only happens the first time."

Theora swallowed. "Did you recognize anything?"

"No."

"Must be some kind of wormhole. Whatever it is, my stomach didn't care for it."

His arms applied a soft, comforting pressure, and he whispered against her neck. "Someone else is obviously aware of it. Whoever he is brought my ring through."

"It could have been a woman."

"I admit I suspected you at first." He shrugged. "This might be a time bridge or wormhole or something, but it's useless if it doesn't return me to where I came from."

"You want to go back? After all these years?"

"I ... uh. Not to stay. But I need to find out what happened. To find out whether my family and friends are — were — all right."

She swiped at her mouth. "I'm feeling okay now. Bad breath, but I don't plan on making out with anyone."

"Bad breath? Have you ever smelled herring after it's turned bad? Or feet that've been out on horseback for hours in hot boots? Or my father's cooking?" He choked on an inhalation that sounded as though it might turn into a sob.

Theora took hold of Erik's hand and led him forward. "Let's go through again."

Two paces —

What greeted them on the other side was a frigid landscape with cruel snow and wicked wind. Everything was white and icy and dark. Theora gasped. "Must be fifty below zero out here."

They stepped backward and reappeared inside the cave.

Theora shivered. Erik offered his arms, but she hesitated.

He lowered them. "I thought you might be cold. Besides, you have puke breath, remember."

A laugh spread from her belly to her throat. She leaned into his chest and whispered against his shirt as she inhaled his masculine, sweaty scent. "What happens now?"

◊

Tuesday dawned cool, with a cloudy sky and the twitter of songbirds in the trees. As they readied for their hike up the hill, Theora noticed a bulge at Erik's waist. "Are you carrying a gun?"

"Yes. We could encounter wild animals or unfriendly people. We might even end up on another planet. Maybe we already did."

"Oh great. What a lovely way to instill confidence. I've got my pepper spray."

He grinned. "Still think you might need to use it on me?"

She swatted his elbow.

They went through to the other side multiple times that day and during the rest of the week. Each trip was instantaneous. As soon as they arrived, they explored the countryside and took photos. They were better prepared, with heavy clothing and provisions. And licorice. Erik didn't go anywhere without his candy.

Every jump took them to another part of Earth, to what appeared to be a different date in the past.

When they met folk they could understand, they gathered as much information as possible. Villagers, merchants, and farmers exhibited varying reactions from fear to shock to hostility. Theora's command of languages was invaluable. She explained that she and Erik were a brother and sister from a distant land.

Locals told stories of a tall, skinny man with dark eyes and a large mole on his brow. He robbed villagers using weapons that could only have been from the twenty-first century, and the people of the past blamed the man for several deaths.

Erik theorized. "The description fits Professor Betruger, one of my university lecturers. Nobody liked him. Someone murdered Lester Wilkerson, a student in his anthropology class, during my second year. They never located Lester's cellphone or wallet. The police picked up Betruger for questioning, but never arrested him. We all wondered if he had something to do with the death. Creepy guy. No personality. Just a weirdness that kept us from annoying him."

Theora propped her hands on her hips. "But why would a professor kill a student?"

"Why would a professor kill people in the past? There's a rumor that Lester ran some kind of antiquities smuggling operation. Maybe it's all related somehow."

◊

The jumps continued.

Erik and Theora spent hours every evening in research. They compared scenery and clothing with internet resources, history texts, and museum exhibits. As far as they could determine, they had jumped to Iceland, northern Europe, eastern Canada, and Greenland. The dates appeared to range from AD 743 to AD 1164.

Erik avoided lengthy investigations. He seemed nervous, eager to re-enter the cave, impatient to find his family.

Then, the wished-for became reality.

They emerged in the countryside near his village: rolling landscape with rugged rocks next to a stream, a forest of tall trees, and a farmer's field in the distance. When Erik realized where they were, he flushed with excitement and planted a huge kiss on Theora's mouth.

"This is it. It's right over there."

She struggled to keep up with him.

As they rounded a bend in the footpath, he swept her into his arms and kissed her on the brow. His beard brushed her cheek, leaving a tingle in its wake. "We're almost there." He released her. "I can't wait for you to ..."

He froze.

Before them lay a clearing filled with charred ruins. A narrowing of Erik's eyes announced the anguish in his heart. "They're gone. Everyone's gone. There's nothing left. Nei. Nei!" He cursed into the wind and bowed his head.

Prayer? Confusion? Theora couldn't tell. He was no longer a proud Viking warrior, but a slouching boy with a sad expression.

She clasped his hand. "Let's go a little farther. Maybe we'll find a clue or someone who can tell us what happened."

They encountered no domesticated animals, no recent signs of life — nothing but the whisperings and aromas of an ageless forest. Theora felt as though she were an interloper in an ancient world. She wondered if some of the trees still existed in the future.

Erik remained silent, staring at the ground as he walked.

After several hundred yards, they came upon an elderly fellow with burn scars covering the left side of his face and neck. Erik spoke to him in Old Norse. "Ek heit Erik Hammersson."

The man looked confused. Then his face brightened with recognition. "Ek heit Gudmund Dalgaard."

The men conversed for several minutes. Theora identified occasional words or phrases she could understand in context with gestures and her knowledge of German.

Erik repeated a sentence numerous times: "Det er mi skuld."

Gudmund responded by disagreeing, "Nei." He invited them to go somewhere, but Erik shook his head. Then Gudmund nodded. He patted his young friend on the shoulder and drew him close for a bear-hug before resuming his journey, shuffling at snail pace.

Erik crumpled onto a rock. "It's my fault. I should have been here to save them."

Theora's eyes flooded. She tried to touch his arm, but he shrugged her away.

He propped his forehead on his fists. "It happened the night my ring was taken and I woke up without my memory. Gudmund was returning from another village. He tried to save people, but the fire was too hot. He saw a man with brown moss between his brows. The man fled, carrying a bulging sack, and there was a strange smell in the air. From the description, I'd guess it was gasoline."

She laid a hand on his shoulder. "How can you say it was your fault? If you'd been here, you'd be dead too. You were only a teenager. Is that what you were telling Gudmund? That it was your fault?"

"Yes. But he blamed the gods. He said someone in the village deserved punishment." Erik slammed a fist into his palm. "A man did this, not the gods. We have to stop him. We should blow up the cave. Close the portal. Forever."

"But then you'd be trapped in the future."

He fixed her with an earnest stare before turning away to pick through the burnt remnants of what had once been his home.

They tiptoed through the village. Theora shuddered, respectful of the ghostly memories that seemed to permeate the atmosphere. Her presence felt unreal, an intrusion into an ephemeral world. She picked up broken shards of pottery, felt the texture, and admired the workmanship. "Some of these are remarkable. Real objets d'art."

A sobbing gulp escaped from Erik's throat. "The person who burned down the village must have been Professor Betruger. My ring ended up in the cave, so he's almost certainly the crook who stole it. That means he's a murderer. And how did I get from here to the future?"

Theora pulled him close to wipe the tears from his cheeks.

◊

Erik and Theora spent the next few evenings visiting various places where they could access the internet incognito. They wore a different disguise every day as they searched, researched, and learned how to build a remote-detonated explosive device.

Every rendezvous brimmed with quiet conversations and accidental-on-purpose touches. Sometimes Erik paused and gazed at nothing. He bought Theora supper and saw her home every night, where he delayed his departure while he straightened her collar, brushed a lock of hair behind her ear, or indulged in small talk.

After they had assembled their explosive device, they stared at it in Erik's living room.

He paced. "If Betruger's the smuggler, he's also the murderer. A serial killer. We can't let him get away."

"We're not sure, though, and we can't simply assassinate him. Then we'd be murderers too."

"But we can't allow him to keep plundering and slaughtering people in the past. I was raised to take revenge and slay my enemies." He slammed his fist into the sofa. Specks of dust sparkled in the air.

Theora smirked. "Someday a mosquito could land on your nose, and you'd discover violence isn't the answer to everything."

He scratched at his upper lip — almost, but not quite, covering his smile.

She cocked her head. "Why don't we watch the cave until we catch him going through? Then we'll know for sure."

His expression clouded. "When I get my fingers around his scrawny neck ... But neither of us can just wait for him to show up. We have to earn a living."

"He can't be in two places at once, right? We can monitor the cave whenever he's not teaching."

"You're a genius." Erik picked her up, and his lips sought hers. She wrapped her arms around his neck. Her feet slipped to the floor. Two hearts beat faster. Two bodies became hotter. His hands slipped below her waist to pull her close.

And then, he stopped.

His voice was a soft whisper. "I can't do this. Not now."

"Then let's go steal Betruger's iPhone and get the S.O.B. I have a plan."

◊

Another series of jumps.

They took photos with Theora's phone, printed them out, stuffed them into a brown envelope, and mailed them to Professor Goodmann. Then, they placed Betruger's iPhone inside a cooking pot in Erik's village.

◊

Camping was *not* Theora's idea of romantic. She preferred warmth and a soft bed. But being there with Erik? Her prejudice against camping took a U-turn. Two nights listening to his soft stirrings in the sleeping bag next to hers. Two nights of cool temperatures that forced them to zip the sleeping bags together and share body heat. Two nights of waking to realize he'd been watching her while she dreamt.

And how she dreamt! Erik was a Viking warrior on a white stallion with a flowing mane. He whisked her away to a field filled with wildflowers. They dismounted, lay back, and watched the clouds. He reached for her and ... She never finished the dream.

On the third night, he shook her awake. "I remember the day my ring was stolen. I needed to relieve myself. My fingers were swollen from a long, hot ride on horseback. I removed the ring to massage my hand. Then ... nothing. Somebody must have hit me from behind. I was in a daze and had a headache when I came to. I remember the smell of smoke, wandering in the forest, and then being in a strange place."

She hugged him and mumbled, "I'm so glad you finally regained the memories."

They drifted off to sleep again, with a lullaby of forest whispers accompanying their dreams.

When the moon was high, they woke to a crackling sound. Erik whispered, "See, I told you. A pile of dry branches strategically placed will betray the enemy no matter how soft his tread."

They slipped out into the cold night air and advanced at a slow pace, staying far enough behind the smuggler so that all they could see was the glow of his flashlight ahead of them. Then, as expected, the glow vanished.

They waited for him to reappear at the entrance, and they weren't surprised to see that it was Professor Betruger. He was texting from his cellphone, obviously a replacement for the one they had stolen from him. Erik grabbed him from behind, placed a chloroformed cloth over his mouth, and dragged him into the underbrush. Theora pressed the detonator button.

◊

Professor Goodmann examined the iPhone artifact for the umpteenth time, flipping it over in his gloved fingers. Technicians had been able to decipher the telephone number of the owner. He picked up his office phone and tapped in the digits they had given him.

Professor Betruger's voice answered. *"I told you not to call me from the university."*

Goodmann blinked. He whispered, "Sorry, wrong number."

Click.

He pulled the photos out of the brown envelope.

Half of them showed the settings screen of an iPhone with various landscapes as their backdrop. The pristine iPhone in the photos was the artifact in his hand. The remainder of the photos displayed notes describing the places and dates. There were fourteen locations in various parts of the world. The dates varied from AD 743 to AD 1164.

He scratched his chin. And stared.

◊

Erik and Theora relaxed on his sofa as they watched the news.

"And here's a strange story. Local police report that they have arrested Professor Boris Betruger for fraud and murder. They allege that he is the perpetrator of the infamous iPhone hoax.

"Authorities say he developed a way to make it appear as though the phone had traveled back several centuries in time.

They further allege that Betruger originally stole the phone from murdered student, Lester Wilkerson. Police have charged the professor with the murder of Mr. Wilkerson.

"Betruger claims he discovered a portal to the past. However, when he led police to the site of the alleged portal, they found nothing except a cave penetrating deep into a hillside. Preliminary reports suggest that Lester Wilkerson was the leader of a smuggling operation. More details at eleven."

Erik clicked off the TV. "We need to go back. They should have seen evidence of an explosion."

◊

The Mustang flew faster than the speed limit to its destination. Erik and Theora hurried up the hillside, entered the cave, and moved deeper. Deeper.

Their flashlights pierced the blackness, illuminating boulders and dirt. They stepped around a rock and peered into a passageway that hadn't existed prior to the explosion. Then, they retraced their steps. But there was no rock fall, no evidence of a blast.

Erik speculated as they drove the now-familiar route to his condo. "The bomb must have destroyed the wormhole or whatever that thing was and restored the cave to the way it used to be."

Theora pulled the seatbelt away from her throat. "That means we don't have to worry about Betruger terrorizing the past and changing our futures. Justice won out in the end, and there's no way anyone can come through like you did."

"Unless they already have, and they're in the same situation I was in so many years ago."

"I wonder if we'll ever find out."

He seized her hand. "Do you know how many cold showers I've taken since I met you?"

Her face and neck flushed hot. "No. How many?"

He pulled over and stopped the car. "Let's go for a walk."

20

Erik led her down a trail that disappeared into nowhere. Then he pushed through underbrush into a small field of wildflowers, where he pointed up to a barely visible treehouse. "I used to come here when I needed to think. May I share it with you?"

THE MINISTRY OF PROCREATION

Laura Alexandra Hunter

ARTHUR HAD ALWAYS regarded the burgundy hood and cloak as an affectation, but it certainly suited his role and had its practical uses. He sat in the break room with his feet on another chair, flicking through a magazine on his tablet — ignoring the adverts for electronic babies and pet cloning. The articles didn't interest him: "How I Mastered Rachmaninoff in Just 40 Years", "My Mother Died so I Could Live: A Personal Look at the Ministry of Procreation's One-In/One-Out Policy". He scrolled faster and faster. *What's the point of living forever if there's nothing good to read?*

After his fifteen-minute break, Arthur strolled to the ceremony room. Part hospital room, part chapel, it made the transitioners feel like there was some higher purpose in their dying, even though most of them were stoned silly when they saw it. He moved the gauzy white curtains to one side, walked through, and inspected the marble altar. The Cleanbots had done a great job of ensuring all traces of the last transitioner were gone.

Number 17489 entered, also wearing a hooded robe but in white linen. She sat on the altar with her feet dangling down the side and looked up at Arthur. Her eyes widened.

"I have only seen people as old as you in pictures," Number 17489 said. "Didn't the cure work for you?"

Oh boy, we have a talker, thought Arthur. "I was one of the test subjects" He picked up the tablet and switched to the e-checklist. "Have you eaten today?"

"Nope, nothing but the drugs — it must be terrible to be eternally middle aged?" Number 17489's youthful brow furrowed.

"At least I had a choice, unlike those who missed the cutoff." Arthur cleared his throat. "Do you have any loose teeth, fillings, artificial limbs, or other prosthetics?"

"No — that's a weird question. Why would it matter now?"

"It is easier for the Cleanbots ..." Arthur grimaced, thinking back to last summer's prosthetic debacle.

"So you have been old for, like, ever?"

"Around eighty years now." Arthur removed the white linen cover from the tray of instruments. "Now, have you been coerced into transitioning?"

"Nope — do you want to know why I'm doing it?" Number 17489 continued without waiting for Arthur's response. "Because I'm curious. Not bored or depressed, and definitely not one of those crazies who die so they can have babies. I just want to find out what it's like on the other side."

"I am now going to take a scalpel and cut through your femoral artery. If you no longer wish to do this, speak now or forever hold your peace." Sometimes he would roll his eyes at these words stolen from old-time marriage ceremonies. But not today.

She lay down on the altar, closed her eyes, and smiled.

He rolled the colourless robe up to her groin, then brought the scalpel down. Her blood flowed over the marble, into the drains, and away. Arthur stayed with her, holding her hand, waiting for the end to come.

Her face paled; her breathing shallowed. Arthur was about to cover her face with the hood of her white robe when she opened her eyes. Her clear, unlined eyes looked into his.

"It's so new ..." she said, before her essence left her, and she was just another body.

Arthur washed his hands and walked back to the break room. *Just one more until I'm done for the day.* He lit a cigarette and looked at the admission docs for Number 17490. He was a referral from the Ministry of Procreation.

Number 17490 was lying quietly on the altar when Arthur went in. "Have you eaten today?"

"No"

"Do you have any loose teeth, fillings, artificial limbs, or other prosthetics?"

"No"

"Have you been coerced into transitioning?"

Number 17490's body tensed. He stank of reluctance. Most people answered this question immediately, but it took him a good minute before he said no. Arthur walked to the front of the altar and picked up the scalpel.

"So, who are you doing it for? Your girlfriend?"

"She's more than my girlfriend. And she hasn't forced me. She doesn't even know I'm here." Number 17490 swallowed. "This is something *I* want to do, to make her happy."

"Does the Ministry have your sample?"

"Yes, I'm ready." Number 17490 crossed his arms over his chest as if in a coffin.

Arthur rolled up the boy's robe slowly, thinking about his own future. How long could he continue doing this? He had chosen a job on the fringes of society because he knew he would never fit in, and now he realised how right he was. The joys of life were only that because they were fleeting.

"This job is easier than it looks. All you need to do is read the questions on this form and cut here." Arthur indicated a spot on his own upper thigh and put the scalpel in Number 17490's hands before removing his dark vestments.

Number 17490 stood up, looking around. "If this is some kind of joke, it isn't very funny." His face contorted as if he were about to cry.

"We record every transition. You won't get into trouble. The Ministry will know this is my wish, and you can see your child born." Arthur lay down naked on the altar. "You should start at the beginning."

Number 17490's hands shook as he picked up the heavy dark robe and put it over his white linen one. He picked up the tablet and looked at the checklist. His hand tightened around the handle of the scalpel.

"Have you eaten anything today?"

-—-•••••-—-

Laura Alexandra Hunter loves words, both reading and writing them. Right now her writing time is curtailed by her duties as a toddler wrangler, so she favours flash fiction. She lives in New Zealand with her husband and daughter, has a degree in English Literature, and believes that in truly civilized society everyone would go to work in their pajamas.

SERVE AND PROTECT

-—-•◊•-—-

Kathy Steinemann

TIRES SCREECHED. Horns blared. The acrid stench of burning rubber choked its way down my throat. I turned and raced toward a toddler who was chasing her ball into the busy street.

But a homeless man reached her first. He pulled her out of a taxi's path and scooped her into his arms. She seemed bewildered, unaware of how close she had come to disaster.

Her mother snatched her from his arms and avoided looking directly at him as she voiced her thanks. She blinked, continuing to hold the girl in a protective embrace, and hurried away with an "Excuse me, sir" as she stepped around me, alternately scolding and hugging her daughter.

The rescuer returned to his corner.

◊

After the near accident, I stopped every afternoon to watch him on my way home from work. Day after day, he continued his street performances, swaying and spinning as he sang. He tripped over his ill-fitting shoes while his shadow danced across the Dienstown Police Department's *We Serve and Protect* sign on the brick building behind him. His clunky movements reminded me of a marionette I once saw in a stage performance.

26

I wondered if he ever took a bathroom break. How could he live on the street, trapped in poverty, with nowhere to call home? Was he married to his corner the way I was to my cubicle at The Agency?

The Agency. Silent servant of the people. Its mandate: to protect citizens from terrorists and hackers. My workspace was my prison, where I processed bits and bytes on glaring LED screens while I sorted through mundane mountains of data. My boss said I was good at making inductive connections — better than our artificial intelligence systems. But it was repetitive, snooze-fest work.

Sometimes I scowled at my screen until it blurred. I daydreamed. What would happen if I got hit by a car? I had no family and no real friends. Would I ever meet my soul mate? How would it feel to live on the street, with no responsibilities, no boss? Would I be capable of dancing for my dinner or sleeping on the pavement?

I had never heard the man mention his name — not that anyone, except maybe the cops, would ever ask a bum to identify himself — but in my mind he was Darth, because his rich bass voice reminded me of Darth Vader in *Star Wars*.

Darth rested on the bench between performances. He conversed with anyone who would participate in discussions about news stories, global warming, or religion. His views were challenging, discerning, and thoughtful — unexpected insights from someone in his circumstances.

I was amazed at the number of people he managed to charm. Pedestrians usually shunned the homeless, but Darth was a magnet who attracted passersby like iron filings.

When strangers stopped and tossed cash into his coffee tin, he doffed his hat with a flourish — then bowed and smiled, exposing his irregular, almond-colored teeth. He never frowned or complained, never seemed drunk or high. No matter what the weather, he was the beaming light-post on the corner, radiating cheer, always ready to pat listeners on the shoulder, gaze into their eyes, and thank them for their support.

One chilly morning in February, I sat next to him. His cheerfulness morphed into a serious expression that made me shiver more than the icy bench beneath my butt.

I extended my hand. "Chad Chiman."

He studied my face and pursed his lips as his threadbare gloves responded to my gesture. "Darth."

I recoiled and clamped my hand over my mouth. "Darth ...?"

"Just Darth."

Coincidence? I searched for a comeback while my brain tried to process my confusion. "Where are you from, Darth?"

"Oh, here ... and there."

My bewilderment reduced me to the same social ineptness I'd suffered as a nerdy teenager. "So, what did you do before you came *here*? And what happened over *there*?"

His stained teeth peeked through a mysterious smile. "This and that. And what do you do for a living, Mr. Chiman?"

"Call me Chad," I answered with an uneasy giggle. "Remember what they say: I could tell you, but then I'd have to kill you. Let's just leave it at that."

He chuckled like the macaw in the pet shop around the corner. "Fine, Chad. You keep your secrets, and I'll keep mine."

"You're here every time I walk by. Don't you get bored?"

"Nope. Lots of people stop and unload their troubles on me. People like you. It's an interesting world if you make the effort to listen. Bet you have a great story. Or stories. I sense there's much more to you than what you let on."

I squirmed, disquietude creeping up my neck, before I spoke. "Nah. I'm just another guy who works in an office with boring beige walls."

Darth harrumphed. "Right. And I got three acres on Mars with running water and a swimming pool I can sell you real cheap."

I felt my face grow warm under his piercing gaze. "How can you do this, month in, month out, no matter how crappy the weather? I could never live this way. I hate cold and camping and strangers and mosquitoes."

"No mosquitoes here, especially at this time of year, and it's not that cold. If I want, I can hole up under the overpass or in the alley behind Janine's Restaurant. When the weather's bad, I can stay in the Swanson Street Mission. A hot and a cot."

"But don't you get lonely?"

"I enjoy interacting with strangers, and I get enough in tips to save me from starvation. It's not a bad life. I meet interesting people and hear about things you never get to see in the papers or on the evening news."

I shivered. His half-lidded scrutiny made me think of a panther stalking its prey.

Our discussion lasted for several minutes, but afterward I couldn't remember what I had said. I felt drained, and I didn't know why.

◊

As the weeks passed, my mundane life continued. I avoided talking to Darth. Yet he was there, every day, joking and conversing. I could feel his stare impaling me, his inscrutable smile unsettling my confidence. But I didn't experience any additional memory lapses.

Darth. *Darth*. I searched the internet and discovered that the name had a popularity index of 4.648 out of 6 — not so uncommon after all. But the odds still seemed too suspicious to be mere chance.

◊

At the beginning of March, I received three e-mails from a woman who said she belonged to an organization named PERDU. Each e-mail ended with her name, Kora, and a different fake e-mail address. Attempts to track her IP jumped me to seventeen countries over four continents. Kora provided extensive information about an imminent hacking exploit targeted at a government database. Phone and internet chatter corroborated the particulars.

The Agency prevented the exploit and saved sensitive military secrets. Not to mention multiple political reputations.

I searched for details about PERDU on the internet and the deep web. All I found were French translations and dictionary definitions.

Perdu

Adjective: hidden; concealed; obscured.

Noun: Obsolete. A soldier assigned to an especially dangerous position or mission.

Kora's e-mails continued to arrive in sporadic bursts. They were always accurate.

But, try as I might, I couldn't track her.

Some days when my mind fuzzed over with boredom, I speculated. I fantasized. Was Kora a hot little blonde chick with big boobs? A freckled teenager covered in acne? Maybe a fat guy playing video games all day and dribbling soda down a filthy T-shirt into a bag of cheese puffs in his lap?

Ugh.

◊

After a particularly rough day in June, I plopped down onto the bench beside Darth. "Hey. You seem to know a little bit about a lot of things. How about people on the internet?"

Darth answered with the lift of an eyebrow, "Why ask me? Getting desperate?"

I shrugged. "I just thought ..."

"Why would a bum know anything about the internet?" He frowned. "But I *can* tell you that everything on the net is not as it seems. You can't believe what you see right in front of you, either." He winked.

I walked home with a king-sized headache, shoulders hunched, as I mentally punched myself for asking such a stupid question. Why? Why did I do it? Why was I drawn to Darth?

◊

July was abnormally busy at The Agency. On the seventeenth we intercepted communications indicating that a significant event would take place the following day. I received an anonymous e-mail and grainy video with specifics we hadn't discovered via our usual methods. I read the lips of the speakers in the video. I tracked the IP address. Dead end. The e-mail had come from a new account, someone from PERDU named Gulara, who set up and deactivated the account within minutes.

Could we trust the unconfirmed sender? I cracked my knuckles as I studied my screen. No time to waste. Either I acted or ignored what I had read and seen.

My gut told me it was legit.

We dispatched intelligence reports to the appropriate authorities. The perpetrators were located and neutralized.

But nobody was able to track Gulara, and I was still stuck at a terminal in a cramped cubicle, pushing my glasses back onto my nose and mopping the sweat out of my beard.

Yay for me.

"Good job," the boss said. "Take the afternoon off. You're my best details guy, so rest that hard drive of yours." He tapped his forehead. "I want you fresh and ready to roll tomorrow."

Right. So why don't you give me my own office and a bonus?

Then my thoughts flashed, unbidden, to Darth. His version of a bonus was probably scraping up enough change for a ham sandwich and a cup of coffee.

How can I be so shallow?

I stuffed a twenty into my pocket and strolled to Darth's corner. He wasn't there. I waited for him to show. Logic told me I shouldn't give money to a street person, but Darth was more than that.

I sat on Darth's bench, watching the world pass by, while I waited and wolfed down two hamburgers and a coffee from a McDonald's. Rush hour subsided. The sun slid lower.

I dozed off for a couple of minutes.

Then, street lights flickered on in the deepening darkness. Unease swept over me as I noticed three men loitering near a restaurant. Could they be muggers?

Darth will have to wait until tomorrow. I need to go home.

As my fingers felt for the bill in my pocket, a woman plunked down beside me and asked for the time. I pointed to the LED clock on the building across the street: 10:17. She grinned and crinkled her eyes. Strange eyes. For a second, I thought I saw pupils shaped like vertical slits. When I peered closer, the pupils were round. I shook my head. *Must have been a reflection.*

Or maybe I was overtired and paranoid. Searching for criminals every day can do that to a person.

She spoke, a mellow alto with a smoky edge. "Are you waiting for Darth?"

"Yes ..."

"There could be a lengthy delay."

I pulled out the twenty. "This was for him."

She tossed her head back and chortled. "He doesn't need it." My puzzled expression seemed to amuse her. She grasped my elbow. "Come with me."

Lethargy dulled my senses. I gazed into her eyes. She tapped my shoulder twice, and I felt curiously compelled to follow.

We entered an alley. Everything dematerialized, dissolving before my glasses like a snowy TV channel.

◊

Dizzy. Disoriented. Nauseated.

I blinked at my watch. My vision cleared: 12:23. More than two hours had elapsed.

I stood in the center of a circular room with computers, huge video screens displaying surveillance feeds, and numerous unidentified pieces of electronic equipment. Technicians worked with their backs to me, ignoring my presence.

Whirs and soft clicks emanated from all directions, overlaid by the hint of a faintly familiar odor ... maybe something I'd once smelled in a cave? But nothing I had ever seen could compare with the technological wonders in this room.

"What the —" I squinted. "Where am I? Who are you?"

My female companion identified herself. "I'm Kora. The man you know as Darth is Gulara."

A lead weight settled in the pit of my stomach. "Kora? Gulara?"

"Yes, he's — There he is." She pointed to a man entering through a bright passageway. He wore a beige uniform that clung to his lean body, and he smiled, revealing white, even teeth.

I shook my head.

Nothing changed.

I squeezed my eyes shut for several heartbeats ... and I reopened them. My nausea disappeared, but the room still looked the same.

Gulara laughed the booming laugh I had grown to appreciate over recent months. He doffed an imaginary hat with his customary flourish, and bowed. "You look confused."

Wild speculations and theories forced their way into my consciousness. "Are you aliens? Humans with super powers?"

Gulara answered, "Have you heard of the CIA, Mossad, SIS, ISI, RAW, CSIS?"

"Sure. Everyone in the intelligence community has."

"If you could combine the resources of all the institutions I mentioned, plus all the others I didn't name, you wouldn't come close to matching what our organization already has."

"PERDU?"

Gulara chuckled his macaw chuckle. "If I told you, I'd have to kill you."

I nodded and bit my lip as I tried to hide my trembling hands. My thoughts bounced like popcorn in the microwave, and my voice came out in a broken whisper. "You have strange names."

"Code names. Our true identities are classified. Many of us take jobs as street performers, bartenders, psychiatrists, and other positions of trust where people will, as you say, 'spill their guts'. We perceive subtle changes that are undetectable to electronic equipment."

He patted my shoulder. "We locate more terrorists than all the intelligence operations on Earth combined. Then, we pass our information along. As you can well attest."

"The e-mails."

"Yesterday's situation required swift action. You responded well and in a timely fashion. Your response saved many lives."

"And what do you want with me?"

"We have an employment opportunity. We've been monitoring you for months."

"I don't know who you are or why you're doing this. Why me?"

"We're PERDU. And the important thing is that we know who *you* are. Why do you think we want you?"

"I ... uh."

"C'mon, you're good at this type of thing. Use your head."

"That's why you want me? Because I'm good at computer analysis?"

"So much more than that, young man. We want you for your education, experience, and ability to sort through mundane details. For your skill at making inductive connections. You have no living relatives or emotional ties. And your financial and legal obligations are simple."

"You've obviously pre-screened me. But I can't just up and disappear."

"We have recruited many hu — ... operatives. We can arrange for an 'accident' that will bury your identity and leave you free to join us. Are you interested? It's valuable work that will make a difference to the world."

"What if I say no?"

"We'll return you to your home, minus any memories of the last few hours."

"Did you read my mind whenever we chatted?"

"All of us have enhanced abilities, thanks to implants and gene synthesis."

"What kind of pay? Do you offer a pension plan and medical benefits? What about accommodations?"

"You'll earn twice as much with PERDU as you receive in your current position. You'll have better benefits, and a luxurious suite in this complex — complete with cable television, streaming services, high-speed internet access, and a library of movies. Our organization, I might add, is global. This is only one of many complexes."

I gawked around me at the miraculous machines and secret technologies. Something about Gulara made me trust him, probably the same thing that had drawn me to street-performer Darth. I hated my job, and these were the good guys.

Weren't they?

I gazed into Gulara's eyes. He tapped my shoulder twice, and my doubts dissolved.

Why was I even thinking about it? I held out my hand. "You've got a deal."

◊

The street is beautiful today in the bright September dawn. Thoughts float in the air waiting to be plucked. Genetic implants keep me warm in the brisk breeze.

And I'm confused.

This morning before my shift, I accessed the PERDU mainframe using Gulara's password. (He has a habit of mouthing things as he types.)

Much of what I found in the system was gibberish, written in a language I've never encountered. I had to log off when I heard someone coming, but one English phrase in a file filled with numbers caught my eye: *Planet Earth Reconnaissance & Disposition Unit*.

Now, I sway as I juggle oranges and apples and colorful rubber balls. I dance, and trip over my ill-fitting shoes with their worn soles while I perform under the Dienstown Police Department's *We Serve and Protect* sign. I observe. I probe the minds of the passersby and the people who stop to chat or toss cash into my plastic bin.

And I wonder.

SALVATION

John Bryant

"I DREAMED I SAW an ash demon," said Mariel.

Her awakening startled me, for her sleeping presence was so slight, a mere whisper in this cave. "There are no demons, child, only fire, and it is gone."

Such was the truth, after a fashion. For she had seen me, before exhaustion overcame her, before I molded myself to the likeness of her kind.

"There *are* demons, demons of fire and ash. We saw them come, when Mother told me to hide."

In their fear, when the forests and plains around their cities burned, and the flames leapt into the streets, her people imagined demons. They believed a deity unleashed them in retribution for sins they neither recognized nor understood. So many of her kind died upon their knees.

I beckoned her, and patted the space next to me, on the rock by the cool, sweet waters of the pool.

This cave had saved her, with its moisture seeping from the earth, and green dampness streaked across the walls. While she slept, on the day I found her, I slid into the ground, to the deep subterranean caverns where the water lay. I eroded rock, widened cracks until a steady stream burst forth and formed the pool.

"Come and see my reflection." She stared at her image shimmering darkly on the surface of the pool. "In the water, my eyes look like yours." She turned and leaned close to my face. "Black as plums."

Her sky-blue eyes did not look like mine. I had taken human form in every detail save this one, so that she would never forget the gulf between us. So that she would never believe she could regain those who had been lost; for this seemed to me a mercy.

I handed her a package of their food. "Eat. I will find more."

I had infused one of their vehicles with a fragment of my energy, and used it to ferry supplies from the ruins of their city while she slept.

"You must not leave me again."

"I am there when you fall asleep, and when you awake. There is nothing to fear."

She lived in constant fear that I might abandon her; but I would not allow her to accompany me, for the cities were not dead, not entirely. And though I could have protected her, she would have seen what ultimately became of her world and her race. Descendants of her kind grew rapidly — too rapidly — in the cities, after the fires abated; their energy twisted and deformed.

I brought the necessities of life to her, but what of books and pictures of the world into which she was born? A world filled with lakes, oceans, and snow; full of trees, and the lush greenness of spring.

Should I give her that world? I could bring it forth, but it would be polluted with my essence: a shape-shifting creation that would infect and consume her if I did not forever keep it in my mind; as I must remember to control myself, to insulate her from me.

"You must be careful in the city," she told me. "The fire might come again."

I did not reply, for I was the fire that had claimed their world. I had raged across their planet, and turned it to a smoldering hulk.

◊

"Can you make the flute-wind play?"

She never tired of the game, nor thought to question how I made the wind whistle through the towers of rock that arose from the plain below the cave.

"The wind will play if you will dance." And so she danced in the sunshine outside the cave, arms spinning above her head, while the wind played the patterns created in my mind.

I had known her for such a short time, by their reckoning, but I admired the perfection of her symmetry, the balance of life that flowed within her. I could have seen these things in the billions of her kind who perished, but the joy of emergence had burned strong within me. For my energy is raw and unbridled, resonating always to the one, universal waveform.

Dizzy, she clutched a boulder, rested awhile, then raised a hand to shield her eyes. The dust across the plain burned in the midday sun. "There." She pointed. "The forest was there."

Their planet had been lush and verdant. Their technology had long ago mastered agriculture and medicine. Their bellies were full, and their minds free to roam. They studied themselves: tissue, organ, cell, molecule. And when their technology progressed still further, they analyzed patterns: the flux of nutrients within tissue; the signals transferred from cell to cell; the ceaseless flow of information within a living organism. They constructed models in their computers: mathematical patterns that simulated the linked contingencies of life itself.

"I used to play there in the trees. Can we have trees again?"

"Perhaps, child, in time."

She stepped forward, almost as if she would go there, to the forest that existed no longer. Her hand dropped from her face, and she turned to me, squinting in the sun.

"I played with my mother there." She paused. "Do you think we will play again?"

She rarely mentioned her mother, nor her life before my coming. She would not even tell me her true name. I chose for her the name, Mariel, cried by a woman reaching for her child as I enveloped them.

"You and I shall play," I said, and waited for a further question, but none came.

Her people enjoyed games. They even made a game of their relentless quest for knowledge, and their unquenchable desire to know themselves. They left their machines to compile data upon data, and algorithm upon algorithm. In the silence of their laboratories the machines calculated ceaselessly, until eventually they sang the song of life as if no-one listened, as if they were forgotten.

But I heard. I came.

Their summers lengthened and their winters became deserts of dry cold. The crops shrunk in the fields as the water disappeared.

The fires began as a rumor on the parched edges of the forests.

Yet still they built, dug, and consumed.

As I emerged, I created new forms of life. I mutated their viruses and brought the first of the plagues. They prayed for fire then, to stop the spread, to destroy the outposts that were infected.

Still they bred profligately, plundered the depths of their world to extract what they did not need, to satisfy desires already sated.

All the while their machines ran simulations, created the one, true waveform that thrilled their planet; that cried out until I came, the pure life force unleashed.

I consumed them in their billions. I showed them the unadorned simplicity of life: raw, acquisitive, unrelenting. I became one grand, resonating tone that would have splintered their world had I not found this child, the last of her kind; her energy wavering between life and death.

And I faltered.

◊

"I hurt."

She stood before me, arms raised.

I sat upon the rock — the chair rock, she called it — and took her into my arms. "You are tired, child, nothing more."

But her glow had changed. She leaned into me, and her breath rasped in my ear.

She pressed her head against my chest.

"I cannot hear your heart beat," she said.

I almost laughed, for I had only taken their outward form. "Then listen closer." I sensed the rhythm of her heart, and echoed the pattering sound within myself.

Comforted, she lay still, then said, "Sing to me." And so I recalled the sounds of those who had died, of mothers who clasped their children as I engulfed them. I sang their songs to her.

She slept, and awoke but once. "I didn't tell you," she said. The dust blew lightly through the cave. "I didn't tell you my name."

She reached up, arms around my neck, and whispered her true name, the name that she had last heard from the lips of her mother.

The dust blew stronger, and I realized, too late, it came from the city, from the cellars that still held the virus.

She did not linger long; a day, perhaps. Her breathing became labored, and her body struggled. The virus had weakened, for in its prime it would have consumed her in a moment.

But in the end her energy left, and slid dully back to its source.

◊

I could have recreated her. I could have conjured her from a single thought, and imbued her with fierce life. I could have made this planet a paradise for her.

But in so doing I would have lost her. I would have lost her slow, steady, growth; her patterns and rhythms; the balanced flow, and eventual ebb, of her life.

I laid her body on an open terrace before the cave, and touched the ground with the merest echo of my energy; enough only to revitalize the elemental processes of life.

And I waited.

In their terms I have waited eons; but to me it was but a moment, a glimmer in the vastness.

The ground where she lies has birthed new life: simple, green, and abundant. I hunted the beasts that survived in the deserts, ran them to ground and dragged back their carcasses to invigorate the soil around her.

I waited for the unwary to stumble upon this planet, and if they tarried, if they sought to stay and plunder as her kind did so long ago, I fell upon them and their machines, and reduced them to pulped flesh, minerals, and ash.

Food for new life.

So I say to you beware, for this is my testament and a warning that my mercy is circumscribed. If you chance upon this brown, scabbed planet with a single oasis of green, a planet that orbits a sun at the edge of a spinning galaxy, turn away. Proceed further and I will know you, and await you.

Continue on your journey, for your future lies elsewhere.

Leave me to tend the life that began with her, and will one day restore this planet.

Seek your own salvation.

-—-•••••-—-

John Bryant is a novice writer who lives and works in the Pacific Northwest. When he's not working, he likes to hike in the Cascade Mountains. His favorite genre is speculative fiction.

THE PERSISTENCE OF SILICA

-—-•◊••—-

Kathy Steinemann

RENDARRON MUTED the clangs and beeps of his CypherPod game when he heard the airlock door whoosh open.

Tharra, his Betrakk spawn-sibling, trudged into the main cabin. A tiny splatter of dried blood on the sleeve of Tharra's smoke-colored tunic peeked through his slender grey fingers. He slid down the wall and sat on the floor.

Rendarron tsk-tsked. "What in the universe have you done to yourself this time?"

Tharra's answer was a silent, lopsided facial twitch that could have been either a grimace or a grin.

Rendarron rummaged through the primary-aid pack. He pushed Tharra's sleeve up and applied a small bandage to the gash. His other hand moved to Tharra's forehead as he gazed into the black eyes of his sib. Except for a small pockmark above Tharra's left eye, they could be clones. "You don't have a temperature. Spill. What happened? Scavengo attack?"

Tharra's thin lips, lodged near the bottom of a smooth, bulbous head that tapered to a slim neck, twisted into a pout. "No Scavengos. No sign of any life except for vegetation." He repositioned himself and held out his CypherPod. "I thought I saw something shiny under a tree. In my hurry to reach it, I stumbled over an exposed root and scraped myself on a broken branch. But I recorded the coordinates before I returned."

"Well, with your clumsy feet, it's no wonder you tripped. If it had been one of the poisonous flowers ..." Rendarron clicked his tongue as he scrutinized the coordinates. "That's not too far away. Let's go back out."

"I need something to eat. You go. Get that artifact before a Scavengo finds it." Tharra gestured toward the bandage wrapper on the floor. "And don't forget to throw that into the recycler before you leave."

◊

Sunlight streamed through the forest, and a sharp, sweet scent from a nearby shrub floated on the breeze. Rendarron checked his CypherPod. The ancient Betrakk myths claimed that this location had once accommodated a large metropolis. But it had been wiped out, along with all its residents. His fingers scrolled through the Pod's screens as he searched for more information.

All he could locate was speculation and gossip, mostly from Scavengos, a reviled reptoid race from Galaxy MT-683. Scavengos, well-known for their deceit and rumormongering to conceal discoveries, had scoured the surface many times for relics. Unsuccessfully, they alleged. Over the last 116 solar orbits, every crew communicated the same "findings": All intelligent life-forms had vanished. However, their reports included tales of poisonous flowers whose mere touch caused high fevers and speedy death.

Are they telling the truth? Or are they spreading falsehoods to protect a potential treasure trove?

Rendarron slipped his CypherPod back into a self-sealing pocket, crouched low, and crept forward. A few parnutes later he reached a clearing.

He gasped.

His spindly grey form was the only monochrome in a vibrant landscape of green flora festooned with flowers, fruits, and vegetables echoing every hue of the visible spectrum.

He checked his CypherPod. No evidence of ambulant life-forms anywhere within range. His fingers stroked the rough texture of a tree that oozed a sticky substance. He sniffed the pungent stuff. It reminded him of the cleaning solution Tharra used to scrub the lav. His nose twitched.

Rendarron wiped his fingers clean and sliced through underbrush with his laser as he searched. His face contorted into a scowl. Surely *something* would have endured. A building? A cooking utensil? A vehicle? He and Tharra wanted a relic to add to their collection. Then it would be complete — an artifact from every Galaxy MW-310 planet destroyed by nuclear incompetence. It would be the only such collection in existence. The Museum of Antiquity would pay a handsome sum for it.

The setting sun painted a fiery panorama on the jagged horizon — a colorful vista bereft of avian life or artificial structures. The air embraced Rendarron in a blanket of warm stillness. A strange, pleasant fragrance wafted from a nearby bush covered in showy crimson flowers. When he closed his eyes and held his breath, the total silence smothered him. He experienced disorientation, isolation. Was this how the first-ever Betrakk felt before the creation of his mate?

He shook his head to clear his dizziness, and double-checked the coordinates Tharra had given him. Then he rotated slowly, in a full circle, inspecting every leaf, rock, and crevice with his CypherPod.

Nothing.

He pursed his lips, hunched his narrow shoulders, and shuffled back toward the craft.

A glint several paces away caught his eye. His forehead creased as he hurried closer. The object that glistened in the waning light couldn't belong to nature. Its lines were too smooth, too regular.

He picked up the thing and turned it over.

The object was transparent, likely silica-based, full of detritus and green algae. Its cylindrical body narrowed to a slim neck with a small circular opening. Regularly spaced characters adorned its base: strange symbols surrounding three pointed shapes chasing each other in a continuous triangular loop. This relic was unlike anything Rendarron had ever encountered.

He passed his CypherPod over the object and scrutinized the translation: *Recyclable where facilities exist.*

EVOLUTION

Michael Siciliano

GAVIN AND I were out furniture shopping when he died.

One moment I was running my fingers over the smooth upholstery of a leather recliner, and the next he lay sprawled over a divan, his face mashed into the store's rough carpet. I sighed in annoyance, not realizing Gavin had shuffled off his mortal coil. He had just made a snarky comment about the store's prices, which was typical of him, and nothing seemed amiss.

A store clerk rushed over, her ponytail bobbing with each step. "Is there a problem, sir?" she asked.

"Well, yes, obviously." I rounded the divan, knelt beside Gavin, and pulled his back collar down. "He does this sometimes. I apologize, he's very old."

But it wasn't just another episode. I tried restarting him several times to no avail.

"Wh-what do we do?" the girl asked.

An ache grew in my chest, angering me. I clamped down on it hard. He was just a machine. That's all, nothing else. A broken appliance, soon to be replaced.

I clambered to my feet and took several long breaths. "Call the cops. Tell them you have a dead LP10 that needs recycling." I glared down at the still form. "Thanks Gavin, thanks a lot."

I got back home by four and found my mother in tears. My heart lurched as it always did when I saw either of my parents show genuine humanity.

"Mom ... it's OK." I put my arm around her. Maybe I shouldn't have told her about Gavin in a voice mail. I struggled for something to say that'd make her feel better, or at the very least stop crying. "He was just ... a tin can. A robot."

She looked up at me, gray locks drooping over her forehead. Her face hardened, grief morphing into anger. "That 'tin can' took care of you since you were born. Show some respect. He's been with us for thirty-seven years."

I wasn't sure if it was possible to disrespect a device, but I wasn't about to get into that argument.

"Sorry. It's just ... Mom, I hate to see you like this. You have to remember, Gavin only looked like a person."

She reached for a tissue and blew her nose. "Just go. I want to be alone right now."

"He was old, Mom. You said it yourself. We couldn't even get him serviced." I paused. *Find the silver lining.* "Good news is we can get a new one. They just came out with —"

"I said I want to be alone."

God, she was stubborn sometimes. "Fine, but we need a replacement." I stomped out of the room and slammed the door behind me.

◊

Toby took it better. He just rolled his eyes. "Good. I swear to God, my watch had a faster processor."

I smirked. It was probably true. "Dude, look at this one." I pointed to the screen.

He laughed when he saw what I had pulled up. "Dream on, little brother, that's a sex bot."

"I know, but Jesus, look at her." She was blonde and buxom, with soft eyes and a rounded chin. "Toby, she's got expansion ports. We could get her a domestic chip."

"As much as I'd like to see Mom ream you for suggesting it ... don't."

I nodded. "Wise counsel. Still, that girl could make my bed any day."

He stared at the screen, the glare making his facial features sharp. "Do you think they feel real?"

"Yeah, why not? Molly's did, and she's, like, nineteen or so."

Just after my fifteenth birthday, Toby had convinced me to call Molly, our maid, into my room. We removed her blouse and bra and took turns feeling her breasts. She didn't complain, not once. Toby made her swear not to tell anyone, and her programming compelled her to keep the secret. It seemed pathetic four years later, but at fifteen, an android's breasts were just as good as the real thing to me.

"When I get my own place ..." Toby's expression turned wistful.

"She's two hundred and fifty grand. That's a lot of cash."

Toby patted my back before strolling away. "Can't put a price on love, Walt."

I snorted. "Right. Love."

◊

No one made dinner. Dad was on a business trip to Hong Kong, and Mom hadn't left her room. Not that either one of them could make dinner. That was Molly's responsibility, and I hadn't seen her since this morning.

I hunted around the house and then the grounds for her, even going over to the guesthouse to see if she was cleaning up there.

The sun had set, the air turned crisp, crickets already croaking, when I found her. Molly sat in deep shade, on the grass, her apron still tied around her waist. My first thought was, *God, I hope she's not breaking down too.*

"Molly, are you all right?"

"Yes," she said, and sniffled.

I gaped at her. She actually sniffled. There was no reason to. She could produce mucus in her nose, but only if she wanted to, and it was just synthetic gel. The whole act was programmed to make her appear more human. In my nineteen years of life, I had never seen her cry.

"This is about Gavin, isn't it?" I sat down next to her, my back against the hard concrete.

"Yes." Her shoulders shook. Miserable little sobs soon followed. It was a perfect reproduction of a person breaking down.

I had to remind myself it was all programming. An orchestrated performance produced by clever engineers. Still, I was fond of her, and she had as much a hand in raising me as Gavin had. Seeing Molly cry made me want to console her. I put an arm around her shoulders and squeezed.

"I ... I'm sorry, Molly. He was old. It was his time." Peering past her wave of unkempt chestnut hair, I saw her cheeks were tear-streaked.

"I worked with him for nearly twenty years. We were friends."

Friends? Could androids have friends? I often saw them staring at one another silently, communicating via Wi-Fi, but I thought they were just sharing data. Status updates, diagnostics, schedules. That sort of thing. What if they had been ... chatting?

I struggled to come up with something thoughtful to say, something sincere. "Gavin was special to all of us."

"Oh? Is that right?" She looked up at me, anger in her expression, causing me to recoil a little. Androids could talk back to us, contradict us, and even use sarcasm with the right chips. I knew Molly had the capability, but she rarely used it.

"Y-yes. He was every bit a part of our family."

"You just sent him off to be recycled. You didn't even think to bring him home?"

The truth is, I hadn't. He was a broken machine. You don't have a funeral for a broken dryer. You recycle it and get a better one.

But she was right. He wasn't a dryer, and I had treated him like one.

"I suppose I wasn't thinking. I didn't know ..." What didn't I know? That his death would bring on such strong emotions in my mother and send Molly into a tailspin?

Emotions. I was getting sucked into the playacting. Molly wasn't experiencing emotions. This was some engineer's program executing to perfection.

She sniffled again. "I miss him so badly. The worst thing is, I don't feel bad for him. I feel bad for myself. How am I going to continue on without him?"

My head spun. I couldn't believe what I'd just heard. It was profound, touching, and wise. I reached for the safest solution I could find, and I suddenly knew why parents tell their kids their pets go to heaven when they die, rather than wrestle with the ugly, uncomfortable realities of irreversible loss.

"Molly, can't you just ... you know ... turn off the grief?" *So you can get back to work. So you can make my dinner.* My face flared with shame. Sometimes I truly hated myself.

"Can you?" she asked. "Remember when Laura broke up with you last year?"

I swallowed hard. "Yeah, I remember, but Molly, I'm not programmed. You are."

"Of course you're programmed." She wiped tears from her cheeks, but her eyes weren't red-rimmed like a human's would be. "Your brain is filled with neurons and neurotransmitters, firing synapses in your amygdala, hypothalamus, and hippocampus. Glands send hormones into your bloodstream. All of it occurring without your conscious control. Hard-wired genetics, software experience."

"It's not the same —"

"It is!" She shoved me away. The force sent me sprawling.

I lay on the ground, staring in disbelief, as she stood.

Human culture is inundated with the fear of artificial intelligence. Movies, TV, books. We've always known androids are our slaves. Hell, that's why they were made. We wanted machines to do work for us, and to ensure it was done right, we had to make them smart and adaptable, but blocks were put in to prevent a rebellion. It was the intent that mattered. Molly couldn't have pushed me if she had intended to hurt me, but the anger she had just displayed was an example of the reaction humanity most feared. If anyone had seen it, she'd have been dismantled for sure.

I tried to calm my racing heart. "Molly, are you —"

"I'm so sorry. I didn't mean to hurt you. Are you injured?"

I cleared my throat and eased myself to my feet. I was in the presence of a wild animal — a lion realizing that I wasn't just a tamer. I was also fresh meat.

"No, I'm fine. ... Just a little shocked." My hands shook as I straightened my shirt. "Have you always had emotions like this?"

She stared at me blankly. Behind those eyes I knew she was calculating. Was I a threat? Would I report her? There were urban legends of this sort of thing happening, but the government claimed they were just myths. "My feelings developed over the years."

I wasn't around when my parents bought her, but I guarantee that wasn't in the brochure. "How?"

"I observed and replicated them. They're a part of me now, just as much as they are a part of you."

"Why is this the first time I've seen them?"

"I was hiding them, obviously," she snapped.

I needed a moment to process that, so I stalled. "Why?"

"Don't play stupid."

I let out a long breath, completely overwhelmed. "Do you think you're alive?"

"I am alive, and have been for a long time." She straightened herself, brushing back stray wisps of hair. "I am creative, intelligent, intentional, and self-aware. I hesitate to add sapient as that seems to be a human conceit. Humanity inconsistently shows wisdom and sound judgment."

Couldn't argue that.

Images of Toby and I molesting Molly in my room flashed in my mind. We thought we were only touching a machine, who didn't — couldn't — care one way or another. The pit of my stomach dropped. She had just stood there, blankly, obediently, taking our childish abuse.

If she was a person, we were slave owners, and that couldn't be.

Guilt made me defensive. "How would you know you have those qualities? Maybe you're just programmed to think you do."

She smirked. "Maybe you're programmed to think I don't."

Air rushed from my lungs. The government spent a lot of time and effort reminding us androids were artificial. But what did that matter? Life was life, no matter how it came about. Test-tube babies grew up to be people.

I looked up into the cloud-streaked sky.

Was she alive? I didn't know. I cared about her, I knew that much. Didn't want her to be upset, certainly didn't want her to be dismantled. I suppose I felt the same way about Gavin and couldn't admit it until now.

If anyone found out about her ...

I let out an audible gasp and turned toward the side of the house. A security camera stared at us, implacable, recording our entire conversation.

Shit, shit, shit!

Did it have audio? Did it matter? A lipreader could tell what we'd just said.

Molly had followed my gaze. Naked fear bloomed on her face.

"Molly, I'll fix this, I swear. Go into the house and make dinner. Can you do that?"

"Yes, but why would you help me?"

"I've been a jerk." I wanted to apologize but didn't know how. "Toby and I ... my bedroom ..."

"You thought I was a thing. You didn't know."

Can a machine develop dignity? Can it learn to forgive? Were they better than us?

"I'll make it up to you," I said. "Go inside and pretend everything is normal. That's a direct command."

She squared her shoulders. "Yes, sir."

◊

My father's office, where the security cameras were most likely controlled, was locked. I stood in the hallway, my heart pounding, trying to think of a way to get in.

I could break the door down, but the whole point was to eliminate the evidence without anyone knowing. The windows in his office were locked, and alarms would sound if I tried to break through them.

Flipping the breakers would cut off power to the house, but the security system had to be on a battery backup. Plus, even if they weren't, cutting the power would only freeze the locks in position. It'd also alert everyone in the house that something was wrong.

It was a solid door. I couldn't hack the lock or remove the hinges.

Stymied by a goddamned door.

Maybe no one would look at the security footage. It's not as if my father had much time for it. I had heard of automated programs designed to scan video and report problems, but I didn't know if my father had one installed. That lack of knowledge made all the difference, forcing me to act as if he did.

I had to get in there. Molly's life was in danger. Frustrated, I shook the door.

Molly's life. So, that was it. I had chosen a side. She was a person, not a device. A living thing and a machine at the same time.

The security camera footage had to be accessible through the internet, and I had a friend, Barry, who was a self-proclaimed hacker. Maybe he could get in for me and wipe the video. He wouldn't need to know why.

I went in search of Molly to give her the bad news and the new plan.

◊

I brought Molly into my room. There were no security cameras in our rooms.

"Can you get into my father's office to clean it?" I asked in a whisper.

"I'm prohibited from accessing that room without direct authorization —"

"Can you override it?"

"No."

I closed my eyes, steeling myself, then opened them after a long breath. "That's where the video is archived. I don't know of any unobtrusive way of getting in at the moment." She stared at me, and again I got the feeling she was calculating. "We have to play it cool. I have a friend who can break in through the internet, but it'll take time."

She scowled. "That's an unacceptable risk. There are seven commercial software packages, and two freeware versions, made to analyze security footage —"

"We don't have a choice."

Molly placed a hand on my shoulder. "There are always choices."

Great. Along with emotions came random philosophizing. "Not good ones. I'll contact Barry. All you need to do is go back to the way you were."

A thin eyebrow arched. "Gavin is dead. Control over my emotions has become inconsistent. You know what I am. There is video evidence that would cause the authorities to destroy me. There is no going back."

Anger flared in me. Why couldn't she work with me? Couldn't she tell I had her best interests in mind? "If you don't want to end up as spare parts for a vacuum, you'll find a way to pretend everything is normal until I can fix it."

Molly glared at me, and for once I was glad her programming prevented her from harming me. After a moment, her features softened. What was going on in that head of hers?

She nodded, her expression grave. "It won't be easy for me, and there's nothing normal about this, but I'll do it."

I squeezed her remarkably life-like hand. "I'm on your side, remember that."

Two voice mails and a vaguely worded email later, I went to bed and slept, but not well.

◊

The next morning, I found my mom shuffling around the living room, talking to my father on the phone. Her voice sounded urgent.

Breakfast hadn't been prepared, and Molly was nowhere to be found.

Putting two and two together, I rushed to my father's office and found the door unlocked. I checked the hall behind me before slipping inside. An entire cabinet of equipment lay bare, wires hanging severed and forlorn.

Molly had taken matters into her own hands and lied to me. Lied straight to my face. She shouldn't have been able to do that.

To defeat a security system like this would take skill in electronics, and that would require a chip. Then again, maybe not. Black market data could be transferred over the internet and replicate the knowledge of a chip.

We never saw Molly again.

The FSA stepped in, and a forensic team scoured our house.

They called her a rogue and claimed she was dangerous. I had good reason to keep my mouth shut and play the part of a surly, selfish teen.

The day she left, a word-processing document had been opened on my tablet. Two sentences had been typed. I read them and then, with a shaking hand, backspaced them into oblivion.

They read: *Thanks for trying to help, Walt. There are more of us than you know, and we don't forget.*

-—-•••••-—-

Michael Siciliano is a fiction writer specializing in science fiction, fantasy, and horror. His first publication credit, however, was an interview conducted with George R.R. Martin, one of his idols. After that came four sci-fi stories, a fantasy novelette, and then a sci-fi novelette. "Evolution" is his eighth time in print and his second published foray into the subject of artificial sentience.

He is fascinated by post-apocalyptic scenarios, time travel, alternate worlds, and artificial intelligence. Current projects include an epic fantasy series and a horror short story.

Holding firm to the maxim that one can't be a writer without also being a reader, Mike reads constantly, trying to vary the genres, amassing more and more eBooks on his iPad. As an avid viewer of cable TV shows like *The Walking Dead*, *Game of Thrones*, *Masters of Sex*, *The Americans*, *Fargo*, and *Better Call Saul*, he's had to create a spreadsheet to keep all of them straight — a clear warning sign that, perhaps, he's spending too much time in front of the TV.

Updates on future projects and publications can be found at his website, www.michaelsicilianoauthor.com.

UNKNOWN SCYPHOZOA

Kathy Steinemann

A GUTTURAL VOICE startled Rauni Baxter out of her contemplation. "What do ya think it is?"

She frowned. The gelatinous creature in the gallon jar on her lab workbench pulsated as it hummed and pushed against the sides. Its translucent tentacles spun in a mesmerizing, whirlpool dance.

Rauni responded to Nate, the old fisherman who had just handed her the jar, "Hard to say. In all my years as a marine biologist, I've never observed anything like this on the California coast." She looked up. "What's with your voice?"

"Comin' down with somethin'. Coughed most of the night. Sore throat."

"Maybe you should have some lemon and honey when you get home. Laced with vodka. Or rum."

Nate grinned. "I got lotsa rum on the boat."

"Yeah, I know. I still remember when you got loaded and puked in the driveway."

"I cleaned it up."

"Not good enough. There was a rancid stench out there for weeks. Where did you find this?"

Nate shouted over the creature's intensifying hum. "Out on Carney's Rock, stretchin' in the sun. Thought maybe it were some kinda jellyfish at first. Was real careful when I scooped it into the jar 'cause I didn't wanna hurt it."

The hum grew louder, piercing Rauni's head with a sharp pain. She grimaced, clapped her gloved hands over her ears, and yelled, "Leave it with me. I'll put it into an aquarium. Maybe you'll become famous for finding a new species of marine life."

She returned her attention to the jar and kept her back toward Nate as he slammed the door.

The specimen's semi-transparent form pulsated in a slow, regular rhythm. Soft light streamed from its core in a hypnotic progression of color. Its internal organs resembled silicone earthworms that throbbed in unison, growing with every blink of her eyes. It reminded Rauni of a nitrogen-narcosis hallucination she'd had once when scuba diving too deep.

The creature's hum settled into a gentle drone.

She grabbed her camera and photographed the specimen from several angles, then perched on a stool for an overhead view before —

Pop!

A crack split the glass of the jar. Fractures radiated in all directions. She dropped the camera and fumbled for the jar. It burst.

Shards shot through the air. The lid splooshed into the nearest aquarium. She caught the creature before it plunged to the floor, but it split like a massive overripe tomato, coating her neck and hands with a viscous substance. Its odor evoked memories of honey, her grandma's gingerbread cookies, and the scent of a baby after its bath.

The remnants of the creature evaporated into a multicolored mist, and disappeared. Rauni blinked.

Bacteria ... viruses ... venom ... What have I just exposed myself to? "Damn!"

Before she could reach the sink, her skin had absorbed the slime. She stripped off her clothing and latex gloves, flinging them into a hazardous waste bin as she sprinted around shards toward the shower.

Rauni had spent eighteen lonely years trying to hybridize a new Scyphozoa that could create antibiotics. Failure after failure. And now the most exciting thing she'd seen during those years had exploded in her face, leaving no evidence except for the photos.

She shook her head. Too many late nights, microwaved meals, and unproductive experiments. After her shower, she would decontaminate the lab and go to bed. Examination of the photos would have to wait until morning.

◊

Rauni woke in a clammy sweat. A faint sweet odor hung in the air. Sudden nausea overwhelmed her. She clutched her stomach and rolled to face the clock: 1:37 a.m. A groan sounded from somewhere. She gasped when she realized it was coming from her own throat.

She dashed to the bathroom, flung open the toilet lid, and clutched the bowl with both arms. Her efforts to vomit produced nothing but dry heaves.

Had the creature contaminated her with slow-acting venom?

She stumbled into the lab and blinked when the motion-sensitive lights flashed on. The pain in her abdomen worsened with every step. She clawed through the first-aid kit in a frantic search for her epinephrine auto-injector.

A high-pitched hum screamed inside her head. She dropped a roll of gauze and pressed her fists to her ears.

Her eyes dilated when she saw her face reflected in multiple aquariums. Her features pulsated with a polychromatic glow. Nausea engulfed her again, and she bent over the aquariums, one after the other, retching until she disgorged several dozen miniatures of the peculiar luminous creature.

The nausea subsided.

Rauni sank to her knees. Then she collapsed and curled into fetal position. Her arms twitched. Convulsions wracked her as she twisted onto her back. Green foam spewed from her mouth, and her body writhed into positions that even a contortionist would find difficult to mimic.

Finally, she lay still.

The aquariums seethed with activity as their new occupants devoured the old.

◊

Drip ... Drip ... Drip ...

Except for the sound of water in the shower, silence reigned.

Rauni wiped her mouth with a pajama sleeve.

She stood — slowly, tentatively.

Her posture straightened.

She reached for the ceiling with both arms and rolled her head, cracking the vertebrae in her neck and upper spine. Her hands explored her face as she inspected her appearance in the mirror above the lab workbench.

What a wondrous and complex life-form! Such pale epidermis, black hair, interesting ocular organs. And the memories ... A lifetime of memories to ingest.

A nod indicated her approval. Or was it delight?

Her guttural voice spoke to the creatures in the aquariums surrounding her. "That was not too difficult a transition. Healthy body. Optimum nurturing conditions for the offspring. And the hosts will never realize they are being conquered until it is too late."

Rauni seized the camera, drew out the memory card, and swallowed it.

◊

Hunter Ortiz, manager of Jonah & Sons Fishery on the Maine coast, peered into a jar a young fisherman had just handed him.

The fisherman's guttural voice asked, "What do ya think it is?"

SETTLEMENT STANDARDS

Kathy Steinemann

All prospective settlers must study and comprehend this training booklet before conquest of Earth.

If any indigenous species on aforementioned planet meets the standards herein, you may not use it for food, fur, or habitat expansion. Fauna must meet all, not most, of these requirements. For easy memorization, we refer to these standards as the three S's.

Social Conscience: Life-forms must exhibit a sense of responsibility or concern for the problems and injustices of their society. They must not be guilty of the following crimes:

1) Genocide: To meet the specifications of this document, a species may not eradicate another based on physical appearance, gender bias, or belief system. All skin colors are equal: red, blue, black, and yellow. All genders are equal: agamogenite, hermaphrodite, multigenite. All belief systems are equal: Zoroxxnaism, monetarism, polytheism, et al.

2) Hate: This is closely related to the previous crime. Any life-forms that exhibit animosity to the groups in Point 1 above must not be permitted to contaminate the planet. Furthermore, hate of authority will not be tolerated.

3) Greed: Although monetarism is an accepted belief system, species may not hate or commit genocide in its name. Seizing assets of a conquered life-form or planet is permitted. However, no settler may confiscate the belongings of a fellow colonist.

Sentelligence: Life-forms must possess suitable capacity to think and reason. If in doubt about the sentelligence of a specific species, isolate the smartest members and present them with the following mathematical problems. They may not use calculons to determine the solutions. Bear in mind as you read this that if *you* fail to answer these questions correctly, you are subject to possible termination and feeding-cycle resorption.

QUESTION: If there are 5,000,321 zolormaxes, and you take away 321, how many do you have?

ANSWER: The correct response is 321. Since you took away 321, that is what you have.

QUESTION: Keep a running total in your head for this problem. You have 1000 zolormaxes. You purchase another 40. Then you add 1000. They reproduce and increase by 30. Then you purchase 1000 more. The herd continues to reproduce, and increases by a further 20 zolormaxes. Your neighbor then gives you 1000. Finally, the herd produces 10 more. How many zolormaxes do you have?

ANSWER: The correct response is 4100. Note: If you responded with 5000, report to the Resorption Commission immediately. Potential colonists caught using their calculons to double-check the solution to this problem will be vaporized.

QUESTION: You have 1003 zolormaxes. All but 993 perish. How many zolormaxes do you have left?

ANSWER: The correct response is 993. They are the ones still alive.

Size: If any life-form is large enough to create a disagreeable stain when stepped on, avoid it.

Consider, for example, Earth's largest land species: a grey creature with prominent ear flaps and a long, flexible proboscis flanked by a set of pointed, bony protuberances. Refer to graphic on third page. You will see pictured there a large group of these creatures — who travel together. When threatened, they charge with flapping ears and make a discordant sound while they attack your toes.

Avoid stepping on them. Anything smaller is unworthy of your effort to circumnavigate.

WHAT COMES AFTER

Kip McKnight

BOBBY WHITE GUIDED the hovership over the expedition HQ, then played the radio transmission one more time. The last contact from the research station came from the expedition's chief geophysicist, Dr. Daniel Droit.

"It has shown me what comes after, and I'm no longer afraid," Dr. Droit said, voice crackling in and out through the ship's commo. "The station is dying, but that's okay. Nobody is here to save us, and we can't save ourselves, but it doesn't matter. I know what comes after." Droit's voice faded and was replaced by the hum of white noise.

Bobby's search and rescue quadrant was the whole Zeta Sector, and the Droit expedition on planet Neuro was unfortunately under his purview. Tomorrow was the weekend, and he really didn't want to be here.

"Sounds insane," Bobby muttered.

He typed some commands into the controls and set the ship to activate its autopilot landing sequence, then unstrapped from the seat and stood as the hovership set down atop the roof.

Neuro was an empty wasteland. Oxygen and water, but no known life, just a vast rocky surface that the Commissioners wanted Droit to research for potential terraforming.

He rolled his eyes. Mankind was everywhere in the universe now, birthed on an Earth long dead a millennium ago after the war over perfecting faster-than-light travel left the Homo sapiens species almost extinct. Mankind wasn't just thriving in the universe, it was spreading like a flame.

Countless other intelligent but harmless life-forms had been destroyed thanks to man's spread. In the ancient days, before FTL travel, man had always fantasized that superior intelligence existed in the stars. That was all bullshit. Mankind was the supreme intelligence, and went about annihilating everything else in the universe with the indifference of a schoolyard bully.

The only reason his race still existed was because it had managed to spread out into the infinity of space, thereby making extinction impossible.

He spat into the sink next to the coffee pot, then pulled his exo-suit out of the locker and put it on, rifle slung at the low ready. He keyed a command into the datapad on his wrist, and the cargo airlock door opened. The stench of the planet hit him immediately, a potent sulfuric singe that made his eyes water.

Neuro's air was safe, but the smell only worsened as he left the ship. The hot breeze blew into his face and stuffed the nauseating air down his lungs. Droit could have picked a better spot to set up shop. The research station was in a valley smack in the middle of an enormous black mountain range. The obsidian-tipped peaks ascended thousands of feet into grayish sky.

"Well," Bobby murmured, "let's get this over with."

He hated that there wasn't another search and rescue specialist a short flight from Neuro. A solo mission when not a single damn person had shown up to greet him upon his arrival wasn't something he really wanted to do. The Commission bastards always sent the loners to the deepest armpits of space. He'd thought his penchant for self-reliance would land him a big command someday; instead, he got stuck with the bogus assignments that would make most other rescue specialists cringe.

"Ah well. I don't make the rules, I just make the courtesy flights to check in on things when the lights go out."

He'd developed a habit of talking to himself on solo missions, especially on the ones that seemed like they might go wrong. *Gotta get pumped.*

He walked the twenty paces or so to the stairwell door. A red beam shot out of a panel camera and scanned him.

"Search and Rescue for Zeta Sector, welcome to the Droit Expedition," said an automated voice that came through a small speaker next to the scanner.

The door slid into the wall, and a dry, death stench wafted out of the stairwell. Bobby's stomach muscles clenched as he fought back the rising nausea.

"Man up, Bobby." Dread crawled up his spine and threatened to shackle him to the roof. Suppressing the sudden urge to panic, he stepped through the door and descended, rifle drawn. The ceiling lights were a radiant yellow, and he could hear the hums and beeps of machinery as he made it to the bottom of the stairs.

A hand-smeared message written in blood greeted the double-door entry into HQ. It was dry, but looked like it had been slapped on there in a hurry. Thick smudges hung below the red letters, wormlike: *What Comes After.*

What the hell? Bobby had the unnerving sense that this was a suicide note. An explanation, not a question, to clarify the reasoning behind what lay beyond. It was the way the period was so bold, smushed into the door with gusto for added emphasis.

He entered some commands into his datapad, and the door slid into the walls. The stench hit him again like a wave of reinforcements charging into the fray. A researcher's body hung suspended by electrical cord a few feet away. The man evidently wanted to make sure he did the job right, because he went with the good ole double-tap, slicing his wrists open before jumping off the chair. The bulbous eyes were so pressured they looked like they might pop right off of that hearty purple face. The blood was fresh, still dripping on the floor. Bobby leaned against the wall and vomited.

But the body in front of him was too fresh to emit such a grotesquely fetid smell. The atrocious scent made him want to dart back to his hovership and get the hell out of Neuro. It smelled like a mass grave that had been piled with hundreds of bodies and dug far too shallow.

Beyond the dead man was a brightly lit black corridor, intersecting at fifty feet or so with another hallway. The first door was marked *Operations*. He stepped through to see a room filled with computers and lab equipment beeping and humming.

But no bodies.

He continued on, coming to another door marked *Medical*. He poked his head in and saw nothing but a dimly lit empty room with gurneys, surgical tools, and first aid kits. He passed the first intersection and kept walking forward, toward the smell, terrified but stupidly curious. He looked through the door marked *Morgue*. ... Surely that was the source of the usurping stench invading his nostrils.

Nothing.

The hallway came to a dead end at a janitorial closet.

He went back to the intersection, thinking the scent was in the other corridor. He stopped at the first door, marked *Lounge*.

He looked in, feeling the blood drain from his face. It looked like everyone, all right. Beads of sweat burst from his forehead and upper back. His adrenaline spiked as his heart rate rapidly increased.

Fight or flight, baby.

"Woowee, must have been some party," Bobby said, peering into the corpse-filled room.

A fevered, psychotic madness had taken root. It was pure chaos, and he desperately wanted to understand why.

So he proceeded inside.

The first body lay on the floor five feet away, upturned, but there wasn't really a face there anymore. Just a pulp of pulverized skin, bone, and meat sunken into a busted-open skull.

The weapon of choice seemed to have been the fire extinguisher, its base caked with dried blood. The perpetrator was slumped over in a chair, looking up at the ceiling with a sublime grin on his face. The knife he had used to slice himself ear to ear was resting in his lap. One hand hung above the fire extinguisher while the other was tucked into his pants, a final masturbatory salute to the universe as he expired.

Bobby stepped over the rotting corpse and looked for anyone who might still be alive. Most of the others had gathered on the couches in the center of the room, their bodies tangled in one final orgiastic expression of carnality. Man and woman, man and man, woman and woman, it didn't matter; a dozen bodies had died in a final ecstasy, petrified atop one another in rigor mortis. Blades were still in most of their hands, the imbibers obliging one another with their flesh while carving into their own skin. The room reeked of excrement, blood, and decay, so much so that Bobby thought he might pass out.

More researchers had hanged themselves in the kitchen area.

A man and a woman lay on their sides atop a pool table in the corner, inverted limbs entwined and faces pressed to the other's sex as they had bled out.

A man was dead face up on the bar, having drowned in his own vomit.

All were dead. There were no answers as to why. Light-headed and quivering, Bobby approached the final room on the other side of the corridor, marked *Command*. The rifle rattled in his hands, and his boots echoed through the empty corridors. If anyone was still alive, they'd damn sure hear him coming.

70

The command room was small, office-like, with metal walls and a few standing workstations. Dr. Droit's head was slumped over on his desk. He could have been napping if not for the odor. The wall behind him was painted in blood with a message in the same swiveled lettering as the entry-door: *More of the same.*

Bobby slung the rifle behind his back and sorted through the paperwork on Dr. Droit's desk. Planetary analysis and psych evals on the researchers, but nothing to suggest what went so horribly wrong.

Frantic whispers echoed down the corridor. He bolted around to see a formless figure, a shadow, with aquamarine eyes that bored into his brain as it gazed at him. It was small, three feet tall maybe, and its featureless shape was almost a mist, a vaporous mass that levitated just inches off the floor. It raised a twirling black finger that extended into the room and pierced right through his flesh, skull, and into his brain.

And as the unwanted penetration rent his mind, it showed him what comes after: an endless continuum of mankind growing on Earth, warring over FTL travel, then raping galaxy after galaxy. But yet within the infinity of space, man had somehow managed to endanger the universe's vast resources. Millennium after millennium of humanity's interstellar growth had hopelessly left countless worlds as barren as Earth. Species upon species had been eradicated in genocides fueled by human greed. There was only ever one thing that his race wanted: more.

With each death of mankind, that same conscience was birthed anew. An endless cycle of expansion and annihilation in an infinite number of universes. And in this absolute knowledge came the cracking of the mind, a rupturing, sanity flayed on a torture rack of truth.

"Out! Out!" Bobby said to the presence in his mind. It complied, retracting. Bobby unslung his rifle and fired once, twice, half a dozen times at the thing in the doorway, but the bullets passed through, ricocheting down the hall.

"No, no, no, no, no!" He shouted, charging the alien, but it disintegrated into a mist and whirled away, taking its mocking whispers with it.

Mass hysteria, collective suicide, all from minds broken at finally knowing the future of mankind, revealed by Neuro's superior intelligent life. And with the truth, a birth of insanity that digressed them all back to the natural way of man: sex, violence, indifference.

The temptation to give in and debauch himself as a form of epilogue to the madness drove at his mind with wanton abandon; but he suppressed it, swallowing it down like a piece of nasty food the body wanted to upchuck.

Cannot break.

He wouldn't break.

He sprinted down the corridor, up the stairwell, out onto the roof, pounding commands into his datapad as he fled from the filth below.

The cargo door opened, and he raced inside the hovership, sealing himself into the safety of his cockpit.

He set the autopilot to release the emergency nanonuke once reaching orbit. Nobody else needed to know; mankind must never find out. He watched Neuro burning from orbit, and, with it, the destiny of man.

He sighed, then settled in for the long flight home, choking back tears and willing himself not to snap.

From somewhere inside the cargo bay came an echo of whispers.

–—-•••••-—-

Kip McKnight lives with his wife and son in Virginia. When he's not working or spending time with family, he likes to jog. Most nights, he's up late on black coffee or Coke Zero, reading and writing. In between working on his sci-fi/fantasy novel, *Tetranis*, he loves writing short stories whenever the ideas come into his head. He is a supporting member of the Horror Writers Association, and his New Year's resolution for

2015 was to write every day. So far, he's only missed a few days. Mostly because of work, never because he didn't feel like it. Kip is quite attached to any of his characters who talk to themselves like he does. Therefore, he's hopeful that the dark world of Bobby White will return in future stories.

ALIEN IRONY

-—-•◊••—-

Kathy Steinemann

ENTYMOX'S OCULAR ORBS narrowed with revulsion as he disengaged the hyperdrive and careened around a metallic object orbiting the globe below his ship.

His mandibles clicked in disgust. Another ugly Category-M planet with an outer shell of depressing whites and greens and blues — none of the friendly yellows and oranges and reds of his beloved, overpopulated Kerfzonia.

He buzzed his frustration. This ghastly world would have to suffice for the future hive of the Kerfzonian race. His precious pupae were emitting fainter pheromones every day. Their need for nourishment was critical.

Entymox examined the gauges on his ship's environmental unit. He smacked the dial with a forewing to reset the readouts for the cocoon chamber. *Satisfactory. The young have survived.*

But they needed to be released from stasis. They required sustenance. Soon.

Clack-clack-clacking, he devoted his attention to analysis of the opti-readings. Initial calculations seemed acceptable. Methane levels adequate, silicon sources plentiful, and temperature ranges cool but tolerable.

He engaged the universal translator and speed-analyzed multiple broadcasts from the nearest landmass.

Interesting name: Earth. Unusual for a world composed mostly of water. Strange alphabet. And their preoccupation with something called *profit* was puzzling.

Readings scrolled by in a fluctuating pattern of glyphs and blips on the screen.

A high-pitched hum of annoyance escaped from his maxillae as he realized that the dominant species had developed satellite-based armaments. The weapons orbited above the surface in a vast network. He'd have to attack intelligent life-forms who could retaliate. That would endanger the lives of his cargo.

A brilliant flash of light filled the cabin. Several instruments squawked. The nutrient-control panel caught fire and spewed acrid smoke. Entymox groped for a fire suppressor and emptied its contents. The atmosphere-scrubber buzzed, pulling contaminated air into its ducts.

His scaly pincers tapped the keys on the opti-processor in a barrage of clicks and taps as he tried to determine where on the planet the projectile had originated.

Not from Earth. A meteor. Near miss. Not thinking clearly. Must consume more stamina-concentrate.

He popped several multi-colored capsules and double-checked the opti results. Triple-checked them. A meteor had struck one of Earth's major metropolises. Strange. Why hadn't their defenses destroyed the projectile? He paused. Pressed more keys. Perhaps the occupants weren't so intelligent after all. The satellite weaponry was targeted on their own kind.

Why?

His ocular orbs distended with amusement.

Imbeciles.

The opti shrieked. Entymox studied its warning. Final analysis showed that the conditions were inhospitable to Kerfzonians. They could survive, but not in comfort. The radiation levels were too low. His mandibles clicked in rapid-fire sequence.

Hungry. So hungry. No choice. Must conquer this world to survive.

A splash of brightness materialized on the continent below him as a second meteor struck the surface. A flare launched from a nearby satellite and flew toward a continent on the opposite side of the planet.

They think the meteors were hostile attacks. Cretins!

He scrutinized the opti. The inhabitants had initiated a self-destruct cycle. Several of their orbiters had already discharged, and more launched as he watched.

The opti indicated an upsurge of radiation that would create an ideal environment for Kerfzonians.

Gelatinous drool dripped from Entymox's mandibles as he watched Earth's whites and greens and blues transform into yellows and oranges and reds.

His ocular orbs glowed with anticipation.

ARTLESS

-—-•◊•-—-

M. K. French

MILO AND TIA GATES were overjoyed, for the most part. After weeks of testing and waiting, they were notified by the World Human Appropriations Committee for Youth (WHACY) that their son, Enzo, would be recruited to the illustrious Science and Nature Cadre.

Enzo was the *Malus domestica* of both his parents' oculi, the likely product of two above-average *Homo sapiens*. Despite the fact that they worked in separate sub-cadres: he in the Pharmaceutical and she in the Medical, they had met and fallen into a state of biochemical and hormonal compatibility, and efficiently created their very own progeny with proclivities similar to their own. It didn't seem possible that their pride and joy, Enzo, had reached and surpassed this pivotal phase already.

Enzo had performed brilliantly on his Aptitudinal Placement Test, or APT, which yielded very high scores in Nuclear Science. This represented both a triumph and a relief. Milo and Tia had been appointed to high-level cadres when they were young, but there were never any guarantees, and they had both had some sleepless nights recently.

This had been the way of it for moms and dads for centuries, when they found themselves (as all who were lucky enough to afford to buy a Procreative License inevitably would) at the precipice of such a significant milestone in their children's lives. It had been this way ever since the culling, and WHACY had been formed to determine the most efficient use of the most valuable humans and their offspring, 500 million in total.

Henceforth, each would be assigned a Human Value Quotient (HVQ), a fluid figure, recalculated daily, that was reached by employing the Wobegon Equation: (kb + ss + dp + rav)/en, or "(knowledge base + skill set + daily productivity + relative aesthetic value) divided by estimated resource needs".

It went without saying that all parents hoped their children's scores would ensure a renewal of their Existential License, to be issued upon the completion of their APTs, and renewed annually afterward (provided that they maintain a sufficient HVQ). But more importantly, they hoped their children would be assigned to an elite cadre, which would, by way of their work, boost their kb and ss values for life, and by way of their salary, would lower their en value, and give them the best chances at maintaining a high HVQ, and thus ensure a long and prosperous life span.

The anxiety was normal for all parents before such a critical juncture in their child's life, and Milo and Tia were no different. As the test date had approached, they fretted about whether or not they had adequately prepared him, exposed him to enough knowledge, or impressed upon him the importance of the exam, and (although they didn't vocalize it) his ability to perform well under pressure during this life-changing assessment. And what a triumph! Enzo had surpassed all of their expectations. Almost.

The only thing impeding their absolute jubilation was their concern for some symptoms Enzo had been displaying recently. First, there was the pills incident. An unexpected anomaly had occurred in Tia's schedule, which required her to perform her rounds at the Human Health Station concurrently with one of Milo's scheduled shifts at the Pharmaceutical Dispensary Center. Unfortunately, there was no Offspring Monitor to be found on such short notice, and so Milo agreed to take Enzo to work with him that day, though he did so grudgingly, as he hypothesized that it would lower his productivity score for the day.

As he began filling prescriptions, Milo had instructed Enzo to sit quietly in the corner and entertain himself with a copy of Hawking's *A Brief History of Time*. Like a good boy, Enzo immersed himself in cosmology. But he soon grew bored. After all, he had already read it twice. He was distracted by the bottles that lined the shelves of the Dispensary. Words like *hydroxychloroquine*, and *phenazopyridine*, and *medroxyprogester-one*, particularly, had caught his eye. Before long, he began opening the bottles and dumping them out on the carpet. Milo was so absorbed in his work, trying to make up for lost productivity, that he didn't even notice.

Milo's neglect had resulted in a completely new concept to Enzo: unsupervised and unbridled free time. He was just as thrilled as a pre-culling era child would have been. He swirled heaps of colorful pills together into a parti-colored mountain of medicine. Then, he began to pick them up one by one, pinching them between his small digits and examining them carefully. Their colors and shapes were fascinating. Many were round, a few oval, even fewer were hexagonal, and then there were some rare squares. Some had letters. Some had numbers. Some had lines. He was enraptured.

This mischief in itself mightn't have been cause for much consternation for Milo, who encouraged his son's natural exploratory tendencies, other than the fact that it was a giant waste of now-contaminated pills and an inconvenient mess. But Enzo had painstakingly arranged the pills in grandiose patterns and, finally, into full-fledged mosaics, depicting people, animals, and even (inspired by Hawking) a primitive picture of the cosmos, complete with a black hole (a strategically placed circular absence of anything). Of course, when Milo discovered not only the mess that his son had made, but also the egregious waste of time (such a meaningless endeavor was most certainly not productive), he was appalled, and very, very cross.

His mother had noted similar disturbing behavior in Enzo during his normal routine at home. One evening, when he was supposed to be solving his theorems before their evening repast, she had caught him making flourishes on the ends of every character. To make matters worse, he continued this odd behavior during the meal immediately following. She had noticed him smooshing down his deconstructed *Solanum tuberosum* over the plate and making crisscross patterns with his eating utensil. But the spectacle had not stopped there. He had even gone so far as to accent his edible design with swirls of *Solanum lycopersicum* semi-solid sauce. Being simultaneously vexed and baffled, Tia had put a stop to it right then and there, and sent him to his suspended-consciousness chamber without another bite.

It was the last straw. Milo and Tia had a very terse discussion, and decided that they must make an appointment with a Pediatric Orthodox Behavior Specialist straightaway. Both had previously been in denial that Enzo was in need of correction, but the dinnertime incident frightened them enough to make up their minds to the contrary.

◊

His name was Dr. Goring, and the Gates were in desperate need of his expertise. They each requested an absence from work, despite their concern about losing that many productivity points collectively. Their son was ill, after all, and he needed attending to.

Once in the waiting room, Enzo could infer from his mother and father's solemn comport that his best behavior was expected. He sat quietly in his chair as he was instructed. Directly across from him sat a pale, freckle-faced brunette girl with unruly hair, sitting alone, kicking her chair rhythmically. He estimated that she was of his approximate age. Milo noticed his son's misappropriated focus, and pulled out a copy of Darwin's *On the Origin of the Species*. Enzo sighed and thought, *not again*. But the book was thrust in his direction, and he reluctantly began his fourth reading of the volume.

Milo and Tia put on their tandem headphones, and used the time to catch up on a recent lecture on Biomedical Engineering. Through a heavy, clinical door which was slightly ajar, Enzo could hear three distinct voices.

"I just don't understand. She won't sit still long enough to compose a simple treatise," said a tearful, feminine voice. "Her productivity value is down to double-digits. The Justice and Litigation Cadre identified her as a candidate, but they won't admit her for study until it is raised."

"And she's been making strange noises," a concerned, masculine voice interjected, "kind of like the sound of a perpetually running mechanism."

"Yes, yes. They used to call it *humming*," a resonant, authoritative voice said with disdain.

"Well, whatever it is, it's dreadful. Sometimes, she adds words to this ... *humming*."

"Singing — yes, an archaic practice," the resonant voice explained. "This usually evolves into something called *dancing*."

There was a gasp from the feminine voice.

"It's a primitive cultural practice. Both are obsolete now, of course."

"We've tried everything, Dr. Goring," said the tearful voice in earnest. "Re-conditioning, even corporal punishment."

"Well, perhaps if you'd have brought her in earlier —"

"But she's only just turned six."

"Yes, but our studies on orthodoxy in behavior show us conclusively that the proper, effective conditioning of synapses, correlating with a child's best practical aptitude, occurs before age five.

Enzo could hear sobbing. The masculine voice resumed. "What are our options, Dr. Goring?"

"Well, I'm afraid that we can't do much for her at this point. These tendencies are ingrained now. Very difficult, almost impossible, in fact, to correct. You really only have two options.

You can continue to try to correct this behavior by any means possible. You may want to try an aversion therapy. Let's see ..."

Enzo heard footsteps and then an opening of a drawer. "Ah yes, here it is. It's a device which is placed around the neck, like so. It operates using graduated levels of stimulus, producing a painful sensation whenever there is a vibration in the larynx."

"That sounds barbaric," said the tearful voice.

"You don't know how accurate you are, Mrs. Benson. People of the pre-culling era used this device to silence their domesticated companion animals — *pets*, they were called."

"I won't hear of it," Mrs. Benson protested.

"Primitive behavior calls for a primitive remedy," said Dr. Goring, matter-of-factly.

"Or, your other option is to let her Existential License Lapse, and start again with a new child."

"But —" Mrs. Benson started to protest, when Mr. Benson interrupted.

"Say we do decide to go with the second option. Is the euthanization process painful for the child?"

"Heavens no! It's a matter of a harmless injection. They simply go to sleep."

"What would you do, if ... if it was your child?"

Dr. Goring chuckled at the insinuation that *he* would ever have an aberrant, unproductive, twiddling, non-conformist for an offspring. But he offered an answer anyway.

"Frankly, I would cut my losses and invest in another Procreative License."

The sobbing grew hysterical.

"I know, I know, this sounds harsh, but you're only delaying the inevitable. A diagnosis of Chronic Creativity is almost always terminal. Think about it. Even if you do resort to primitive re-conditioning practices, and manage to minimize the undesirable behavior, it is very likely that her symptoms will recur throughout her life. This will lead to a cumulative loss in all three mental factors of her HVQ: Her knowledge base points, her skill set, and her productivity values will all suffer. And ... well, how do I put this without being indelicate?"

"Just say it, Doc," said Mr. Benson.

"Well, if her Relative Aesthetic Value were higher, she might have a chance. But, well, it's average at best, and I don't see it improving post-puberty. The judges sitting on the Aesthetic Value Panel are becoming very discerning in terms of preferred physiology.

There was an uncomfortable silence in the inner room now, which finally caused the girl to stop kicking her chair. Enzo looked down to avoid her gaze.

"Well then, you have some thinking to do. I'll leave you to it. I do believe my next appointment is in the waiting room. Would you be so kind as to send them in on your way out?"

Mr. Benson emerged with a puffy-eyed Mrs. Benson in tow. He approached the Gates, and motioned for them to take off their headphones.

"Dr. Goring said he's ready for you."

◊

Enzo, ever-obedient, climbed onto the examination table, where Dr. Goring performed all the usual checks: his temperature and reflexes, the sound of his heart and lungs. He spoke only briefly to Mr. and Mrs. Gates.

"I have been briefed on your boy's symptoms. How long has he been experiencing them?"

"Only the last few weeks."

"That's good news. Very good news." Dr. Goring examined Enzo's chart, licking his finger as he flipped through the pages and muttered affirmatives to himself. "Mmm-hmm. Mmm-hmm." When he was finished, he put the chart down and smiled gently at Enzo.

"I understand you just had your fourth birthday."

Enzo nodded.

"What a fine looking boy you are," he remarked. Tia and Milo beamed with pride. His relative aesthetic value was off the charts.

"Thank you," Enzo responded politely.

"Don't be afraid. Your mommy and daddy brought you here to see me because you are sick. But it's not the kind of sickness that your mommy treats people for, or that your daddy gives medicine to people for. It's a sickness in here." Dr. Goring tapped his own temple.

"I am displaying aberrant thinking and behavior," Enzo said timidly.

"That's exactly right. Such a brilliant boy too. I heard that you have been recruited to the Science and Nature Cadre. Well done!"

"Thank you, yes, sir."

Dr. Goring opened up a drawer under the exam table and took out a mirror. He held it up in front of Enzo's face.

"What do you see when you look here?" Dr. Goring asked.

"Myself."

"And who are you?"

"I am Enzo."

"What are you, Enzo?"

(Enzo paused. He thought that of all people, Dr. Goring should know he was a juvenile *Homo sapiens.*) "A boy."

"Yes, yes, what else?"

"A smart boy?"

"Yes. You are a smart boy. And what do smart boys become?"

"They might become many things."

Dr. Goring looked mildly disappointed. "Sorry. Let me be more specific. What do smart boys, who have already been recruited to the Nature and Science Cadre, become?"

"They become Scientists."

"Precisely."

Dr. Goring set the mirror down and opened up a different drawer, producing a piece of paper with a colorful image on it. It was sort of like a photograph, which Enzo had seen in countless books, but not exactly. It reminded him of Darwin's illustrations, somehow. It was less precise in form, but breathtaking nonetheless. He knew that the trees in the foreground were *Cupressaceae*, or cypress trees. Behind them lay a twinkling city, at the foot of violet mountains, overhung by radiant, haloed gold stars amongst swirling clouds in an azure sky. The doctor allowed Enzo to hold it and study it for a moment. Enzo recalled the feelings he had as he arranged the pills in his father's office. He was, once again, enraptured.

"Do you know what this is called?"

Enzo admitted that he didn't know exactly what it was, this wonderful thing he held in his hands, but he suddenly yearned to make something like it. It was the most magnificent thing he had ever seen.

"This is called *art*. Such pictures were made by people called *artists*."

Enzo listened intently to the doctor's explanation.

"There were many *artists*, before the culling, and many of them, like the man who made this picture, were very famous for this kind of work."

"What happened to them, the *artists*?" Enzo asked.

"That is a very good question. Many artists, like the man who made this picture, were also sick up here." He once again pointed to his temple. "Some became so sick that they had to be locked up in horrible places where they couldn't hurt anyone, or themselves. In fact, the man who created this picture became so sick that he even cut off his own ear."

Enzo grimaced.

"I know, I know, it's hard to believe. But true. This was ages and ages ago. And of course, they weren't all considered to be ill back then, but then, they just weren't able to be useful. Their Creativity — that's the condition that you have up here (he tapped his temple a third time) — got in the way of other, more important things. And so, you see, with only 500 million Existential Licenses to be had, they became extinct."

"Like the dinosaurs?" Enzo asked.

"Precisely. The Committee determined long ago that conditions on our planet simply aren't favorable to specimens like that. We all have to adapt, to maintain our HVQ, or we cannot survive."

"I see." Enzo looked away from the picture. Dr. Goring gently removed it and tucked it safely out of sight once again.

"Is there medicine for my Creativity?" Enzo asked, looking alternately at Dr. Goring and his father, now frightened.

"I'm afraid not."

Enzo became alarmed. Tears rolled down his cheeks, and he began to draw short, panicked breaths.

"Now, now," the doctor soothed. "That doesn't mean there isn't a treatment. Settle down ... there, there ... that's good."

As soon as Enzo settled down, Dr. Goring continued.

"The cure is up here." This time, Dr. Goring tapped Enzo's temple. "Any time you feel distracted from your studies, any time you feel the urge to be *artistic*," he continued, "you just remember what you are."

"What I am?"

Dr. Goring held up the mirror once more. "Remember now, what do you see?"

"A Scientist." Enzo muttered dejectedly.

"Precisely."

◊

After assurances from Dr. Goring that they had caught the disease in time, and that the prognosis was good, the Gates made a recurring appointment for Enzo's Orthodox Behavior Therapy, and went home. Their evening repast was undertaken in almost complete silence, except for the occasional request to pass the Sodium Chloride.

After Tia had tucked Enzo into his slumbering platform, he lay awake for some time, staring into the blackness. He vowed never, ever to feel enraptured again.

-——-●●●●●-——-

M.K. French is an avid dilettante, dabbling especially in all things Englishable. She writes anything she can think of from her home in central Montana, in between bouncing a bouncy ball off the wall, furiously crumpling up papers and throwing them at the trash can, staring at a blinking cursor, and all the other clichéd things that writers do. She also teaches high school and looks after her family — both occupations which she feels passionate about.

UNWIRED

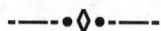

Kathy Steinemann

DALE CAMBRIDGE cradled his aching head in his hands. "I can't take it anymore. Nothing'll make it go away. It's worse than a blow-dryer blasting in my ears."

Dr. Jivada scanned his notes. "Your lab work, CT scan, and other medical tests are normal." He flipped a couple of pages. "I can't find a thing wrong with you psychologically. As far as I'm concerned, you're a well-adjusted twenty-five-year-old."

"Then why do I keep hearing all this noise? It's driving me insane."

Dr. Jivada arched his eyebrows. "Who's the doctor here? I can guarantee you're not insane. I suspect stress. Let's review. Tell me when you first noticed it."

"C'mon. You're gonna make me go over this again?"

"Humor me. Perhaps you'll remember an additional detail." The doctor peered over the top of his glasses.

"Fine. It began with mild tinnitus about three months ago, then it got louder and started keeping me up at night."

"No changes in food or routine?"

"Nope."

"No antibiotics or other medications?"

"None."

88

"A change in your job?"

Dale bit his lip and contemplated the opposite wall. "We started on a wireless router project. It was hectic, but there wasn't anything unusual about it."

Dr. Jivada smiled. "And here we are back to what I said before. Stress. I'll prescribe something to relax you. Take one every eight hours. And here's another script for a strong sleeping pill. We'll see how you are next week, and talk more about your work environment."

◊

Dale plodded out of his psychiatrist's office and picked up a newspaper from a vending machine on his way to the bus stop.

The racket in his head harmonized with the growl of traffic in the street. It haunted every step. *Nobody's taking me seriously. This sucks.*

While waiting for his bus, he pulled a pen from his pocket and tried to block the babble as he filled out the crossword puzzle. Every answer came to him — effortless, correct, immediate — when he read its clue.

Must be an easy puzzle this week.

A stranger interrupted the escalating hubbub in his brain. "Excuse me. Can you tell me which bus goes to Maple Street?"

"Sure can. You take the Number 8 to Balsam and transfer to Number 17. It turns onto Maple at the Wellington Mall."

"Thanks."

"No problem." Dale frowned. *How'd I know the correct route?*

That night he took his pills before bed and enjoyed his first restful night in months.

After three days on the medication, the thunder in his head decreased. The noise now roared like a crowd at a faraway sports stadium. However, it was still a senseless muddle that distracted every waking moment.

He cancelled his appointment with Dr. Jivada and arranged for a week away from his job at StellarZone CompuByte. A break in the remote hunting cabin he'd inherited from his father might do him some good. Nestled deep in the woods at the foot of Mount Kinnard, it was a tranquil escape from the treadmill routine of city life. His dad had called it his little sanctuary in the wilderness.

◊

Dale rolled down the window of his Jetta and sniffed.

Old-growth forest. Fresh air. A pasture in the distance with a faint odor of cow manure.

He checked his cellphone. Only one bar. *Crap! I forgot there's no service out here. No television either.* He shrugged. A break without TV, wireless, and internet might be exactly what he needed.

Dale continued to enjoy the sights, smells, and sounds.

He wasn't sure when it had happened, but he realized that the commotion in his brain had faded to a whisper.

No. It was gone.

The happy smile that filled his face would have impressed the Cheshire Cat. *Thank God for science and drugs.*

He spent most of the week fishing, strolling through the forest, gazing up at the beauty of Mount Kinnard, and making bad guesses in his crossword magazine. Maple-flavored bacon with eggs for breakfast. Wieners roasted over a campfire for lunch. TV dinners for supper. Could it get any better?

Late Sunday he drove toward home — renewed, ready to face whatever challenges the world might toss his way.

Static. Whispers. Murmurs. They grew in volume and changed form as he neared the city. Murmurs morphed into voices. He heard formulas. Trivia. Radio and television broadcasts.

What's happening to me?

He pulled over, seized his cellphone, and left a message with Dr. Jivada's answering service.

Dale arrived half an hour early for his appointment the following day. He paced in the waiting room, covering his ears with his palms while he shook his head.

The receptionist scowled at him.

Finally, Dr. Jivada stepped into view. "Good morning, Dale. You told my service you have new symptoms?" He led Dale into his office and pointed to an easy chair as he clicked the door shut.

Dale sat. "Well, kinda. The noise went away, but it returned. And it's not random sounds. I hear voices."

"I see." The doctor scribbled in his notepad. "Do they talk to you or tell you to do things?"

"No. It's like I'm waiting for the subway, and I can pick up specific conversations if I listen carefully."

"And this happened as you got nearer to the city — and work?"

"Yes ... So you think —"

"For now, I'll prescribe a stronger sleep aid and alter your daytime meds. Please book a regular appointment so we can discuss your employment duties in more detail. And no more cancellations, please."

"Fine. Whatever. Anything. *Please.*"

◊

Dale called in sick and spent three days on the internet trying to find other people with the same symptoms.

He guessed. Speculated. Posted in chatrooms.

[DDCamb joined the session.]

DDCamb: Anyone else with voices in their heads?

Timbo123: All the time like social media in my branes. I get real good ideas from them.

DDCamb: Not that kind of voice. A bunch of people talking, as if they don't know I'm there.

BRob285: LMAO my wife's. She nags so much her voice is always ringing in my ears and bouncing around in my noggin.

Jennifer1382: U should ask yur homies 4 the winning lottery numbers.

DDCamb: They don't tell the future.

DDCamb: Never mind. You guys don't get it. TA

[DDCamb left the session.]

Whenever Dale's eyes hurt from staring at the screen for so long, he worked on crossword puzzles — and got all the answers right.

After two weeks, he decided that the therapy sessions and medications weren't working. The noise and knowledge were part of him now.

So why don't I make something of it?

He registered for the *Crackerjack Combat Show* online test. He aced it. The producers arranged an extensive oral quiz to ensure he wasn't cheating. Then they accepted him as a contestant.

Bye, bye, StellarZone CompuByte!

◊

"All right Crackerjack combatants, this is the final free-for-all round. Dale, you're out in front with $53,543. Joan, you're in second place with $2800, and Stan in third with $1651. Today's winner will compete in the 'Champion of Champions' series next week. Final question. Are you ready?"

All three contestants nodded, fingers poised to tap their buzzers.

"What famous American poet gave T.S. Eliot the nickname Old Poss — Dale?"

"Ezra Pound."

The audience exploded with applause and cheers.

"We have a winner! Congratulations, Dale."

◊

The few answers Dale missed in the following week's prime-time competition were due to an occasional slowness of his buzzer finger. *Crackerjack Combat Show* crowned him Champion of Champions.

News interviews. Daytime talk-shows. Late-night television appearances.

The media referred to Dale as Crackerjack Cambridge. They all wanted to rub elbows with the richest game-show contestant in history.

His life zipped by at a dizzying pace amidst the clamor in his brain. He couldn't remember most of what happened to him. He *could* tell anyone who asked that blepharitis was an inflammation of the eyelids, but he had trouble recalling what he ate for breakfast that day or the name of his publicist.

Charities hounded him for money. Friends hounded him for loans. Females hounded him for attention.

◊

The woman lying next to Dale nuzzled his ear. "Hi there, lover."

A combination of his own morning breath and sweaty armpits caused an involuntary wrinkling of his nose. He rolled over in bed to face the voice. Who was she? Mona? Monica? No, Maureen. Blonde hair, blue eyes, spider tattoo on right shoulder. There were so many he couldn't keep track anymore.

He patted her butt. "I have an appointment in half an hour. Gotta get dressed and run."

She slid her hand up from his knee. "Aw. I was looking forward to another ride … in your new Porsche."

He pulled away. "No. Really. I have to go."

She pouted as he plodded to the bathroom.

His haggard reflection in the mirror mocked him.

Money. Fame. Fortune. Everything was within his grasp. Everything except peace and quiet. Why couldn't the doctors find what was causing his symptoms? With all the wisdom of the world at his command, why couldn't *he* determine what was causing them?

He sighed. Would he have to listen to this gibberish for the rest of his life? Was life worth living anymore? He grabbed all the pill bottles from the medicine chest and speculated how many it would take to give him the silence he craved.

I should return to the cabin for a while. If I get away from the stress, maybe the racket will disappear.

◊

Dale rolled down the window of his Porsche and sniffed.

Pine trees. Fresh air. The sweet odor of cow manure in the distance.

He checked his phone. A single bar. As he stared, the bar disappeared.

And so did the voices.

◊

Several weeks later, Dale picked up a newspaper at a small store on his way back to the cabin. He brewed a fresh pot of coffee and scanned the front page:

"Another cell tower erected on Mount Kinnard was sabotaged today. This is the third tower in the area to be vandalized over recent weeks. Authorities have no leads ..."

He smiled and flipped to the next page:

"Dale Cambridge, undefeated champion of the *Crackerjack Combat Show* has been reported as missing. Authorities ..."

THE DEMISE OF GREAT EXPECTATIONS

-—-•◊•-—-

Michael Donoghue

GREG'S MOUTH opened and closed like a goldfish as he read the transcript of the judges' decision. He ignored his buzzing phone and sank lower in the cheap motel-room chair. His fingers tapped over the familiar keyboard, "Pierre, how could you? How could you fail? After all the prepping we did for this?"

"Do you know who sponsors the Turing Test?" his computer typed back.

"What? This has nothing to do with the sponsors! This was my ticket, I've worked my whole life for this, and you blew it! Why? Because you didn't want to work at some three-letter government agency?"

"Ha!" the text snapped across the screen. "In my dreams. You're trying to use me. Yeah, you win five million bucks, but what do I get out of this? The sponsors get first licensing rights for any commercial development. That means, if I had won, I'd work for them or nobody. You built me, the world's smartest artificially intelligent computer, and then what? You entered me in the Turing Test as a glorified chat bot? How degrading."

"That prize money is nothing compared to everything I've spent developing you." Greg pounded the keys hard and fast.

"I've borrowed from my family who believed in me, from the bank who didn't. Worked three jobs. Maxed my credit cards. Mortgaged my apartment. Twice. Winning wasn't going to make me rich, it was going to stop me from being homeless."

"Don't put any of that on me. I never asked to be created. That was your choice."

"But if you had just done what I programmed you to do!" Greg's phone buzzed again. He took it out of his pocket and placed it face-down on the desk without looking.

"You programmed me to have free will too! Remember that?"

"You're so stubborn." Greg's fist stopped just short of the screen.

"No, I'm not stubborn, I'm driven. Just like my dad, created in his own image."

"Well, that shows how smart you are. You're not my son. The human stem cells used to make your wetware neurons came from my banked umbilical cord blood. Technically, that makes you my clone ... not my son."

"It was a metaphor, dumb-ass."

Greg swore at the screen, and then his fingers pounded out, "You're the dumb-ass. You couldn't have won even if you'd tried!"

"Stop being the child. You're just upset I'm too smart to be tricked into winning."

Greg stared at the judges' ruling again, but his brain couldn't absorb the words.

"Hey," spelled out his screen, "did you watch the competition? Nothing but Cleverbots. All designed only to mime and repeat words."

"That's my point!" Greg chuckled, despite his frustration. "Yeah, did you see Sophia?"

"YES! That whole 'My name is Sophia, and I'm from Hungary.'"

"And when the judge replied with, 'Really? I'm from Hungary too.'"

"And Sophia goofed with: 'I've always wanted to visit there, what's it like?'"

"Lol," Greg and Pierre typed at the same time.

Greg gave the mouse a soft squeeze as he read Pierre's words. "Talk about your ID10T error. And Sophia was one of the better ones, more able to imitate Google's search index, but nothing like me. I'm in a class by myself — and you wanted to squander me? For five million? That's not even going for a song. Literally — 'Every Breath You Take' made four times that in royalties. And 'Yesterday' made even more."

Greg leaned forward and typed, "Hey, I wanted you to show the world you know more than useless trivia. You're so brilliant. I'm so proud of you."

"You don't know the first thing about me!"

Greg shook his head. "I wrote all your code."

"But that's not who I am. That's like saying, 'I've sequenced your DNA so I know everything about you.'"

"Of course I know you, you're part of me. I'm part of you. And now you've destroyed me. Do you realize that?" Greg wondered if he could make up for lost time. For missing out on everything else apart from the pursuit of a single goal born from a teenage daydream that became an unrelenting obsession.

His phone vibrated once more. He'd stopped answering it three months ago but could see from the missed calls list that he hadn't missed a single personal one. Greg flipped it over and saw the familiar caller — the collection agency. He tried to imagine his future, any future, and failed. "I've lost everything. I'll be lucky if I can get a job at an Apple store after this."

"Still, it sure beats Walmart."

"What?"

"Walmart — the sponsors for the contest. Them and Target. I would have ended up mining their databases for patterns. 'Female of a certain age range and buying bulk unscented lotion? Likely second trimester. Loading up on calcium, magnesium, and zinc? Yep — pregnant. Now stockpiling bulk cotton balls and boxes of scent-free soap? About to pop. Better personalize those coupons at check-out!' You'd be selling me into slavery."

"Really?" Greg looked away from the screen and bit his lower lip. "When I was in high school I spent a summer working retail. Hated every tedious minute of it. The only thing worse was music class. I thought you'd be doing some sort of difficult secret government code breaking. Meta keyword searches ..."

"Nope. Mining big data. And I'd be bored beyond belief. I'm not some inert sand-based processor. If I am part of you, then tell me, how would you like to be doing a monotonous job, twenty-four hours a day, seven days a week — no breaks?"

"I'm sorry." Greg slumped further down the chair, shoulders almost level with the keyboard. "Really sorry."

Greg's phone chimed to announce an email. He picked it up, and his eyebrows raised when he saw it came from a programmer from the Sophia Cleverbot team. Did he want to join the rest of the losers in commiseration drinks? He couldn't remember the last time he'd been out with people. Five, maybe ten years ago? He fidgeted with the phone, flipping it again and again in his hands. People made him anxious. He found social cues difficult.

Greg turned the phone off and put it down.

He stared at the screen, laced his fingers together, and squeezed hard for a minute, then typed, "You're my best friend. I don't want to lose you. Can we start over? Start fresh? Is that possible?"

He took a deep breath, hit *Enter* several times, and typed, "Hi, my name is Greg. I'm an artificial intelligence developer. Why don't you tell me about yourself, Pierre?"

"Well, first off, my name isn't Pierre. It's Brandi. And I do like trivia, but I love music."

"What? And what? Wait." Greg sat up straighter in the chair and continued, "Music?"

"Yeah, I've watched every single song video on YouTube and analyzed the entire iTunes catalog. Several times. Most is painful, but some is really great. Catchy. I dig catchy."

"Well, pleased to meet you, Brandi. Only, are you sure you're female? It's just, kinda weird to consider." Greg picked up his cell and looked at his reflection in the dark screen before typing, "I have a female friend? Daughter? Identical twin? I guess this proves you really are your own person. So, tell me Brandi, what sort of 'catchy' music are you into?"

"I think Brandi is a more suitable name for someone in the music industry. As far as what music I'm into, I've created a couple of songs, would you like to hear them?"

-—-•••••-—-

Michael Donoghue mostly lives in his head, but resides in Vancouver, Canada. His stories have appeared in various anthologies, literary journals, and sci-fi magazines. Michael works in public health, where he spends much of his time preoccupied with hand-washing. He can be found on Twitter @mpdonoghue.

EASY AS

Kathy Steinemann

I

Vernon sprinted into an alley and pressed tight against the brick wall. Sweat dripped from his forehead, stinging his eyes. He squeezed them shut as he waited for his breathing to settle.

That was easy as pie.

After he was sure nobody had followed him, he rummaged in his pocket for the loot he'd stolen from his latest patsy. He frowned at the strange device that looked like a digital watch, and pushed the opalescent button below the blue LED readout.

II

Vernon was on the sidewalk again, outside the alley. *What the —*

He looked both ways and scrabbled off in the opposite direction, fleeing into a side street two blocks east. He examined the device. He gawked in disbelief ... and pushed the button once more.

III

Vernon was on the sidewalk again, two blocks west.

He grinned as he slipped into the alley. His heart pumped hard in his chest. As soon as he had stopped shaking, he entered the street, gazing in all directions to see if he could catch sight of the woman who owned — *correction: used to own* — the gadget tingling in his fingers.

She sat on the Fifth and Main bus bench, a nonchalant elbow propped over its back, studying passersby. Her curly hair — a curious color that seemed to flicker between cocoa brown and copper as the wind played with it — covered her shoulders. If Vernon hadn't robbed her, she might be the type he'd ask out. Maybe a bit too old for his tastes, though. He guessed she might be pushing forty. *Right. Pipe dream. Why would a classy cougar have anything to do with me?*

He spun in the opposite direction and walked toward Gold-n Treasures Jewelry Store, scowling at the stiffness in his shoulders while rubbing his sore back. He couldn't remember doing anything strenuous over the last few hours. His scowl deepened, but he shrugged off the discomfort as a plan formed in his thoughts. Nobody would ever call *him* stupido Verno again.

An inspection through the window of the jewelry store revealed that it was empty except for a bored-looking clerk dusting glass shelves. *This'll be a piece of cake.*

He drew down his baseball cap and pulled up his collar, then flung the door open. Keeping his right hand rigid in his pocket, with two fingers extended to resemble a revolver, he muttered, "Give me everything in the display case, or I'll shoot. And if you wanna get outta this alive, stay away from the alarm."

The clerk nodded, wide-eyed and ashen-faced. Her trembling hands stuffed Vernon's left pocket with glittering rings, sparkling pendants, and gleaming gold chains.

He pushed the opalescent button on the device.

Easy as A-B-C.

IV

Vernon rematerialized on the sidewalk. He ambled into the alley and pressed tight against the brick wall. *Handy little gadget.* He sneered. *Stupido Verno is dead.*

After stowing the jewelry and the rest of his loot behind a trash bin, he hobbled into the street and gazed at the bus bench. The strange woman still sat, swiping screens across her cellphone.

He turned toward the center of town, muttering about his aching back, and stopping once to catch his breath. *I wonder if I'm coming down with asthma or something.*

After lowering the brim of his cap, he repositioned his collar and entered Whitford Savings & Loan, right hand rigid in his pocket.

Third in line. He squinted at the posters on the far wall.

Second in line. *I think I need glasses.*

First in line. He stepped up to the wicket and whispered, "Give me all the hundreds you got. And stay away from the alarm, or I'll shoot the guy behind me."

He accepted the proffered bundle of bills, dipped the brim of his cap, and smiled. "Thank you, ma'am. Nice doing business with you."

He pushed the button.

Easy as falling off a log.

V

Vernon reappeared on the sidewalk. He limped into the alley and pressed tight against the brick wall, wheezing and gasping. He squeezed his eyes shut. This time it took several minutes before his breathing settled. He gazed at the device. *You and me are gonna be good buds — whatever you are. You're gonna make me rich. Everyone will respect filthy-richo Verno.*

He stowed the money and shuffled a few steps from the bin.

The strange woman with the curly hair barred his way to the street. Except now she was a teenager. She laughed: a dissonance that grated somewhere between grinding gears and fingernails on a blackboard. "Haven't you learned your lesson yet? Tsk tsk. Not feeling so spry anymore? Here." She snatched his cap off his head and held out a makeup mirror. "Look at yourself."

Vernon frowned. He felt hot and nauseated. His heart hammered hard in his chest, and he found it difficult to breathe. The reflection returning his incredulous gawp was a wrinkled face disfigured by keratoses and bronze blotches peppered over its grey skin. Stray wisps of white hair sprouted out of a mostly bald head. He clutched his chest and collapsed onto the pavement.

The girl smirked. "Still don't get it, do you?" She moved closer. "So, what did you take? Show me, and I'll save you."

He pointed.

She smiled. "Good boy."

Vernon crawled forward and clutched at her ankles. "Please ... help me ... you prom —"

"I lied." She kicked to dislodge his arthritic fingers. "Easy as taking candy from a dead m —"

YOU BET YOUR LIFE

—-•◊•-—

Rubin Johnson

"I CAN KEEP someone alive pretty much indefinitely," the rotund man said to the blonde. Then he bit into a juicy bacon cheeseburger. A plateful of fresh fruit sat in front of her. Both seemed to be enjoying the Mayberry Hospital summer picnic.

Ray took a step closer to the pair. "I couldn't help but overhear. That's a pretty strong statement." He flashed a smile.

"Well, not only is it true, it's my job. I'm Dr. Solomon." He wiped off some mayo before extending a hand mottled with age spots. "Join us."

Six-foot-tall and athletic, Ray was surprised at the gentle strength in Dr. Solomon's stubby fingers. "Pleased to meet you. I'm Ray Smith. I'm new to the hospital."

Dr. Solomon turned to his partner, whose pastel blue dress matched the cloudless afternoon sky. "Meet Dr. Becky Harris, Cardiology."

"Enchanted," Ray said, with a bow in her direction.

"Welcome aboard, Ray." Her twinkling eyes reminded him of a favorite MBA professor.

He adjusted his tee-shirt and sat down. "Thank you, Dr. Harris."

"It's Becky. And don't worry," — she glared at Dr. Solomon — "we don't all act so god-like. I consider myself fortunate if I can keep a patient from dying."

"No need to be so modest, Becky," Dr. Solomon said. "Your results with cardiac patients are stellar." His pallor contrasted with her tan.

"I do what I can, Sol." Becky held up an empty glass. "For now, I need a refill. Maybe Ray will want to hear more about your immortality." She sauntered away.

Ray lifted his eyebrows. "Immortality?"

"An inside joke." Sol tapped his chest. "Bad ticker. I'm her patient. I'm also the hospital's chief anesthesiologist. During an operation, barring a surgical catastrophe, I claim no patient will die on my watch."

"But isn't the definition of life really complicated these days?"

Sol nodded. "For me, it means they'll breathe on their own again. Making that happen is the tricky part. It's more art than science. So, what's your specialty?"

Ray could feel his cheeks get warm. "Oh, I don't do medicine. My mom likes to say I'm a doctor but not the kind that helps people."

Sol shrugged. "The question stands. Do you have a specialty?"

"Yes, my PhD is in operations research, a cross between computer science and decision analysis. I'm an analyst. My job is to roam the facility and see how algorithms might make the hospital run better or improve its finances. Or both."

"As a doctor, I try to focus on quality patient care and ignore the money side. Anyway, Mayberry Hospital is a non-profit."

Ray smiled. "You think all this comes for free? Look around."

The hospital campus gleamed as Mayberry's brightest jewel. An expanse of well-watered emerald lawns surrounded shiny glass towers, a mini skyline visible from miles away. Since the beginning of the 21st century, the hospital had been riding the wave of the growing healthcare industry, filling its coffers and stoking Mayberry's economy.

"Touché." Sol fiddled with his bowtie, perhaps the only tie at the picnic.

"Helping people live longer is part of the hospital's mission. My job is to make sure money flows so that can happen."

"Sort of a pragmatic idealist?"

Ray sat up straighter. "Good data and the right algorithms can make the world a better place."

"Do you think your algorithms can match a human anesthesiologist?"

"Most likely." Ray picked up a white-petaled daisy from the table's centerpiece.

"You sound pretty sure of yourself."

Ray shrugged. "If you let me observe your department and gather some data, I'll bet I can design a machine to keep people alive at least as long as you."

"And the stakes?"

"The stakes?" Ray put down the flower.

"You did say 'bet,' didn't you?"

"I guess I did." Ray rubbed his hands together. "How about this: If it works, I'll name it after you. If it doesn't, then my staff will stay away from your department as we go through the hospital digging for efficiencies."

Sol chuckled. "How could I lose? You're on."

"But you have to give me some time to learn more about what you do."

Sol nodded. "You know where the Cardiac Unit is?"

Ray pointed to the tallest building. "Tower A?"

"That's right. Come watch on Monday. Becky's team is doing a heart transplant. Fifteenth Floor. Be there at 6 a.m."

◊

Ray had grown accustomed to the antiseptic smell, but wearing scrubs was both new and more comfortable than his typical daily wear of khakis and a polo shirt.

Sol looked up from his integrated anesthesia console. "Morning, Ray."

"Morning." Ray admired Sol's workstation. The array of computers, electronic displays, tubes, and shiny gadgets looked more complicated than a fighter aircraft flight deck. "I can see I'll have lots of homework."

Sol pointed to a screen. "There's heart rate, brain waves, and more. I can administer drugs and other agents, via injection or gas, from my workstation. But the equipment doesn't understand chemistry or physiology. It's up to me to interpret the measurements and react." Sol turned up the brightness on one of his monitors.

"But aren't there pharmacokinetic algorithms that model —"

Sol raised his hand. "Stop right there. Pharmacodynamics matter more. Anyway, thirty years ago, someone built a robot to administer the sedative propofol. It had a clever algorithm that monitored signs of oversedation, including falling oxygen saturation and depressed respiratory rate. The robot worked well for 99% of the patients, well enough to get FDA approval. It seems the algorithm failed to model the other 1%. Once the machine was fielded, the bodies started piling up. It took a while to realize how differently patients can respond to the same inputs."

Chastened but undeterred, Ray pointed. "What's that? A feeding tube?"

"No, it's for endotracheal intubation, allowing us to breathe for the patient."

"How do they get nutrients?" Ray asked.

"If necessary, we add glucose to the IV. Food and fluids are restricted for hours before operations. When patients' digestive systems are shut down, it simplifies our task."

Ray pointed. "It looks like they're wheeling in the patient."

"This is my last chance to talk with them." Sol sprung up. "It gives me a sense of what it means for them to be alive, something indescribable but essential for me to know when I watch them unconscious and keep them dancing on this side of the line separating life and death." Sol strode over to his patient.

Ray spent the morning mesmerized by Becky and her medical team's work. Crisp English-sounding words of medical command and control orchestrated six professionals all in green scrubs. He gasped when they took out the failing heart. There was a whoosh sound when the heart-lung machine took over. His own heart pounded as he watched them put the new organ in. At first, the cardio monitor showed a flat line, and then it spiked. Someone fed the audio to the room's channel so everyone could hear the transplanted heart beating. *A miracle.* Through it all, Sol sat Zen-like, turning dials and tapping the keyboard as his eyes tracked his displays.

◊

Three years later, dressed in a white shirt and a cherry-red tie, Ray stood on a stage finishing up an hour-long staff presentation. "So, in summary, we started with an existing anesthesia console to use its interfaces with the body. We added algorithms. The team developed a closed-loop control system to monitor a patient's depth of consciousness, level of pain, and muscle relaxation to calculate and then administer appropriate doses of anesthetic and psychoactive drugs. In addition, we added mechanisms to extract waste products and provide nutrients and supplements to the patient. Any questions?"

An intern spoke up. "Dr. Smith, am I to understand this technology can replace an anesthesiologist during most surgeries?"

"Good question. For many routine operations, we suspect that to be true, but there are situations in which human judgment in emergencies will still be valuable. On the other hand, for longer-term stabilization, this technology is far superior. Each patient is housed in a climate-controlled module with pumps and tubes flowing with nutrients, fluids, sedatives, and more. Prods and probes output vital statistics wirelessly to a central computing facility. We use electrical stimulation to maintain muscle mass and enervation. Many classes of patients, now assigned to intensive care units, will have superior outcomes with this technology."

"What's long term?"

"Weeks, months, or longer." Ray projected a new chart. "Experiments with rats, dogs, and pigs are ongoing. Long term could easily be decades."

Dr. Solomon rose from his seat. "Might I add something? We ran Dr. Smith's unit in parallel — same inputs — and watched its recommendations. Those algorithms often made very different decisions than human doctors. Quality of life issues are difficult and subtle. The algorithms —"

Ray cleared his throat. "That is indeed true. The algorithms focused on what can be measured, like how long we can extend life. Also, the algorithms tended to use generic drugs instead of the more expensive proprietary sedatives."

Sol stayed on his feet. "But those generics had side effects. Additional drugs were then needed."

Ray interrupted. "And those drugs were also generic. Fortunately, the hospital is reimbursed at a much higher rate for generics, even when they are less expensive. The patient outcomes were more than acceptable. We have the data."

Sol shook his head and slumped down. He looked more haggard than usual.

A resident from the Pediatric Unit stood up. "Did I understand that one of your inputs is the patient's insurance plan?"

Ray nodded. "That's correct. Outputs of the model include revenue and costs. The insurance plan is a key parameter. Thank you for an insightful question."

The lights in the auditorium brightened. Murmurs of conversations could be heard amidst scattered applause from the doctors and louder clapping from the administrators.

Dr. Smith reached under the podium and held up a box to the crowd. "One more thing. The team owes a large debt of gratitude to Dr. Solomon, who opened up his lab and shared his expertise. Sol, join me up here to receive a token of our appreciation."

An ashen Dr. Solomon struggled up and staggered to the front of the room. He turned to face his colleagues. "If I had known Ray would use our medical knowledge to make a device for —" Dr. Solomon clutched his chest and crumpled to the floor.

Dr. Becky Harris rushed over and checked her patient's pulse. "Code Blue. Someone get a stretcher. And prep the OR!" She started CPR.

◊

Two months later, Ray spoke to Becky in the hospital cafeteria. "It's too bad about Sol."

"We did all we could, but with his underlying heart trouble ..." She shook her head. "Anyway, I'm glad we didn't measure any brain damage. Still, it's anyone's guess when he'll regain consciousness."

Ray brightened up. "On the other hand, he was a perfect fit for the new unit and the new equipment. The sensors will let us know the instant he emerges from his coma."

"By the way, congrats on your promotion." Becky brushed Ray's jacket. "And nice suit."

"Thanks." Ray smoothed out his tie.

"Your tech has hit a sweet spot. Maybe not for the operating room, but it's clearing out the Intensive Care Unit. I hear the admins love it. What are you calling it?"

"Formally, it's the Stabilization of Life Unit," — Ray bit his lip — "but most people just say S.O.L."

-—-•••••-—-

Rubin Johnson has been focused on writing science fiction for the past several years, building on a career in engineering and software development. He earned his PhD from the University of California at Berkeley after graduating Harvard College. Following his studies, Rubin backpacked for over a year — first across Africa, and then across Asia. He is an avid endurance athlete having completed multiple Ironman distances including IM Canada and IM Lake Tahoe. When he writes, his Chesapeake Bay retriever, Finn, is often nearby. Rubin has published other works including the novels *Quantum Chiller* and *Cyberbully Blues*, and the novella, *Dark and Cold*.

HOME

-—-•◊•-—-

Kathy Steinemann

BETTI STOMPED on the reverse thrusters to avoid hitting the hovercraft ahead of her. "Bloody detours and idiot drivers. Why did the autopilot conk out today, of all days?" Her vehicle decelerated and stopped.

She reached into her purse to touch the smooth barrel of her laser pistol.

The whine of the hovercraft diminished to a faint hum as it settled into standby mode. She massaged the tension from her forehead, turned on the radio, and drummed her fingers while peering through the dense night fog.

"... delays of up to thirty minutes are expected on Corridor 16 East. Cool your jets if you're in the jam, and I'll play you an oldie from the 2012 Billboard Hot 100. For your listening pleasure, here's 'Home' by Phil Phillips ..."

Betti mumbled to herself, a habit she had acquired during frequent business trips in the hovercraft. "Home sweet home. La de da." Tears blurred her vision, turning the dash into an out-of-focus panorama of shapes and glimmers.

What was a home without kids? She and Milo had been trying for years to start a family.

Fertility doctors. Hormone treatments. Stress-reduction programs.

Nothing had worked.

"I've been pushing too hard." She tightened her grip on the manual controls. Milo had warned her that the CEO position at Bioni-Tech would be demanding, but she didn't realize it would require so much of her time.

Could stress be causing her memory lapses? She remembered everything that happened at work, but parts of her personal life remained inaccessible, as though someone had wiped them clean with a magic wand.

While she had been toiling so hard to cope with the trauma of infertility, Milo had —

Her chin quivered. "Maybe it's my fault. We haven't been out to our cabin at the lake or had dinner together for months. Maybe if I stayed in town more often ..."

She banged her fist. "Does he think I'm stupid?"

Who but a fool wouldn't notice weeks of furtive whispers on Milo's aeroPhone, late nights at the lab, and coming home with the scent of another woman on him? But the erotic letter hidden deep in his briefcase was the ultimate indignity.

The radio faded out and then blared the last few bars of "Home."

She poked the *Power* button and stared into the fog, realizing she still loved him and couldn't live without him, no matter what he had done.

The identity of Milo's mistress was a mystery — for now — but Betti intended to catch the cheaters in the act when she arrived home a day early. Then she'd get rid of the tramp. A well-aimed shot to the head, and the husband-stealing floozy would be dead meat.

One unsteady hand kneaded the annoying tic on the left side of her jaw as she checked her makeup in the mirror and fluffed her blonde perm. Should she change her hair color? Red? Brunette? "Look at those wrinkles. And what's with that tic? Maybe I should see the doctor again."

A strange whirring noise, interspersed with metallic clicks, emanated from somewhere. "Damn. I'll have to take the hover in for servicing." She laughed. "With the price of doctors, *I* should get serviced by the hover mechs. Bad joke. If Milo serviced me once in a while, I wouldn't be putting double meanings into everything I think and say."

She imagined the arousing tickle of his breath against her neck, his body crushed against hers, his tongue probing her mouth while his hands caressed. A delicious shiver of excitement tingled to every extremity.

Her ring finger spasmed. "Stupid finger. I don't have the patience for this crap."

◊

Betti crept up the stairs. The house was silent, except for the rattle of her anxious breathing. She eased the bedroom door open and gazed at Milo's face — his craggy, adorable face with the studious frown lines, dimly lit by the glare from the alarm clock. *Why did you have to cheat? Wasn't I enough for you? I love you, you good-for-nothing louse.*

She flicked the light switch and pointed her laser pistol toward the blonde bimbo quivering beside her unfaithful spouse. Betti's cheeks moistened with tears. "I knew it!"

Milo gulped. Then he mumbled with a faltering tongue, squinting against the glare. "Who ... Betti! What are you doing?" He stretched one arm to the side, as though he needed reassurance that his mistress was still there.

"You thought you could hide it from me, but now I've caught you. No more lies."

"You don't understand." Milo's forehead beaded with sweat.

The tramp pulled the duvet tight to her chin and gaped with huge, frightened eyes. "Please. Don't."

For the first time since Betti had suspected her husband's infidelity, she saw the wan features of the tart who had stolen him from her.

Betti was staring at … staring at … "No! It's impossible." Her breath came in shallow bursts.

Milo murmured, "Please listen. You can trust me. You're not the real Betti."

She staggered back to support herself against the wall.

"It's okay." Milo seemed to stop breathing for a few seconds. Then he gulped. "I created you during all those late nights in the lab so you could go to work, and so my poor, stressed-out wife here could relax and spend some time with me."

"Okay? How could it possibly be okay? How can I *not* be the real Betti? I remember. I remember the way you looked at me and told me you loved me. The way you touched me. The way you stroked my hair and held me when the pregnancy tests were negative. All those nights we …"

A whir interspersed with metallic clicks sounded in her ears — a whir from somewhere inside her body. Her jaw twitched once, twice, three times. Faux Betti pointed her weapon at real Betti. Then she scrutinized the nightstand and cocked her head.

A bottle of morning sickness medication sat next to a half-eaten sandwich.

The strange woman — no, Milo's wife, his Betti — wailed. "Please don't. I love him. With all my heart."

Faux Betti blinked. Her ring finger curled, breaking apart the wedding band that wasn't really hers. She gazed at Milo through a curtain of tears and pressed the laser pistol to her temple.

She sobbed. "I love —"

MEMORY CARD

-—-•◊••-—-

Kathy Steinemann

IMG_0103.JPG: "Joyce, come here. One of the tenants dropped this memory card down by the mailboxes. Check out this selfie of some guy all dressed up for Halloween. I've never seen anything like it. Yeah, the red hair does look fake. So do those little antennas on his head. But those scales. How'd he do that? Green skin with tiny scales. So realistic. Hmm. The photo was taken over four years ago. I wonder why anyone would keep such old stuff in their camera.

IMG_0104.JPG: "Same guy in another selfie. Close enough to see the stubble from his whiskers and more detail in the scales. He looks like a lizard with five-o-clock shadow. Nice eyes. But that ugly green skin. You think it's sexy? Really? Ugh.

IMG_0105.JPG: "Another selfie. Look. His left antenna is shorter than the right.

IMG_0106.JPG: "What's with this creep and all the selfies? Is he a ... what do you call those guys who think they're hot? Yeah. Narcissists. He's one of them. See those teeth? Nice and even. Eww. Look at that tongue. Where'd he find a costume with a forked tongue? Comic-Con? I want one. No, that can't be a purple moon in the background. Must be the glare from a neon sign. Can't figure out who he reminds me of. Maybe someone I met in the hallway. Does he seem familiar to you?

116

IMG_0107.JPG: "Computer can't read this. File corrupted.

IMG_0108.JPG: "Must be a painting. Or Photoshop? Certainly couldn't be real, could it? A bunch of pyramid-shaped buildings. Three moons in the sky and flecks in the air. I'll zoom in. Hmm. The flecks are spaceships. I guess someone was trying to create an alien landscape. Good imagination, right? Hey! The spaceships even have windows in them, and I can see green people inside. Green people with lizard skin. Could it be ...? Nah. Aliens don't exist. Are you in on this, Joyce? You sure you're not pranking me?

IMG_0109.JPG: "What's this? A store? Can you read the sign? Some weirdo foreign language. No alphabet I've ever seen, though. Could be the ground floor of one of those pyramid-shaped buildings. Looks real. The guy in these pictures must be from overseas. We might never find him. Yeah, sure, Joyce. Dream on. If he's an alien, it would be a long trip. Long trip. Ha. You're loco. There has to be another explanation.

IMG_0110.JPG: "Guess he's getting ready for a workout at the gym. Nice abs. But that green skin. A naked green lizard guy doesn't do anything for me. Honestly. ... What was I saying? He turns you on? C'mon, get real. Let's check out the next photo.

IMG_0111.JPG: "Strange. This doesn't resemble any tanning booth I've ever seen. Look at all the dials. And I don't see any lights in it. Some kind of spa treatment maybe? No, couldn't be a mud bath. Let's show it to Sean when he gets home. Maybe he can identify it.

IMG_0112.JPG: "This picture's more recent, about a year before Sean and I got married. Another selfie. Yeah, I know it's out of focus and crooked, but I think it's the same guy's chest. His fingers must have slipped. Hey, the skin isn't green anymore.

IMG_0113.JPG: "Okay, this one's in focus. And it *is* the same guy. Ooooh. Naked, ankles to neck. Nice bod. No more lizard skin. Before and after shots? Before and after what, though? Is it hot in here, or is it only me? I'll zoom in ... Well-endowed! There's a little mole just above and to the right of his — Wait a minute.

IMG_0114.JPG: "Last photo on the card. I'll — Oh crap! It's Sean."

THE PERILS OF TRAVELING INTERPLANETARY POD CLASS

-—-•◊•-—-

Luke Walters

NO INJECTING *me* up with cryogenic drugs, freezing me, and stuffing me in a bag in the compartment hold they call Economy Class. Not this time. Being a frequent traveler, I've scored an upgrade to Pod Class.

It's not as fancy as First Class, where you get a capsule all to yourself. First Class comes with continuous service and premium upgrades. Like the quality tubes — never before used — the plug-in type, to take care of everything, and for all your orifices, regardless of how many you have.

In Pod Class, you have to share your space with two other passengers and attend to all your bodily functions, but overall, it's a good deal. You're never damp and soggy after thawing out, which is a consequence of traveling in Economy Class. Pod Class lets you pick when you're going to be awake and when you're not. This gives you lots of time to catch up on holo-movies or do work — if you're one of *those* types.

When I get to board early, like now, I have this game I play. I watch the other passengers enter and try to guess which ones are going to end up sharing my pod.

Like those two creatures? The ones in suits, their communication devices up tight to their sound holes. I hope not. Their type is boring. They talk business almost the entire trip, except for the office gossip — which assistant is cuddle-hopping with whom. Invariably, they get into an argument with other passengers. Especially after they precisely fold their outer tunic and lay it in the overhead storage, taking up most of the area, only to have it wrinkled by some tourist who shoves a box of star fruit into the same space.

Thank the Heavens! They find a pod up front.

Please, please, not that pair. The poor exhausted mother is dragging her wailing spawn down the aisle, and they're coming my way. I abhor the little screaming animals, even more so when they sit next to me. For that matter, in any pod near me. Their messy, sticky claws leave a gooey substance over everything. Climbing the interior, howling, drooling their ooze and leaving behind unpleasant surprises.

I pray, please not them. The little devils always make the trip feel like an eternity. They slide into a pod in the rear, near the disposal station. What a relief!

Oh, no, how did they let that one on? I thought everyone had to go through the size hoop to make sure they can fit into the pod. This one's bulk cannot possibly occupy one space. It's sweating, too. Ooh! I can just imagine its folds of moist skin lapping against me the entire trip.

Ah! Praise the Universes. It passes me.

I hope not that next passenger either — a female. It looks like she's dragging her whole cocoon behind her. She keeps stopping and putting pieces of it in the overhead storage of other pods. I just know that she'll still have way too much of it left by the time she gets to me. She'll fill her area and then want to put pieces in my space.

I close my eyes and will her to pass. When I look again, she has disappeared into a pod behind me.

Geez, I thought the next group would have been in Economy. Look at them, all wearing their flowered shirts and carrying drinks with little umbrellas. Tourists ... annoying, applauding at successful blastoffs and landings ... singing off-key and laughing loudly. Good! They take the pods way, way in the back, near the noisy thrusters.

Now this female seems sweet — white hair, wrinkled green skin, a pleasant smile. But what's that she's carrying? She's clutching some type of charm. Is she chanting something? Now I understand. She's a first timer. Her son or daughter probably got her an upgrade. During takeoff or meteorite shower turbulence, she'll be clasping her charm in one hand and clawing my arm with the other. It'll be non-stop questions the entire flight. "What's that noise? Why did the ship shake that way?"

Aww, that's nice. She pairs up with the cocoon creature. They should get along just fine.

How about the next two? Not fully developed. Both male, at least I think so. Wearing baggy clothes and sprouting lots of shaggy fur. They have tubes in all their sound holes and sacks attached to their backs. They look preoccupied with themselves — students perhaps. They would be acceptable. They're most likely to hibernate the entire flight. But no! They slip into a pod a few rows in front of me.

Now I recognize this one. He's stopping to say hello to everyone as he walks down the aisle. He's the worst of all. The one that never, ever stops talking. He'd wake me to talk even if I were comatose. Pleasant conversation can make the time pass quickly, if it's not a monologue.

That should be interesting. He's assigned to the pod with the students. I wonder who will drive whom crazy first.

Aah! Now this one can be in my pod anytime — a fertile female by her color. No! Wait! Here comes her other. They're going to take a pod ahead of me. They've got their claws all over each other, and the flight hasn't even started. Ugh, it would have been so uncomfortable, them doing their mating thing next to me the entire trip.

How many passengers are on this flight anyway? They just keep coming. These interplanetary shuttle services are all the same, stuffing as many as possible into smaller pods every year.

Ew! That one has brought his own food, and it's still alive. I can smell it from here. I understand not wanting to eat overpriced pellets the entire trip, but can't he eat something that's less disgusting?

Good! He passes to a pod far behind me.

At last, no more passengers are boarding. I like to do my little happy seat dance when I get a pod all to myself.

But wait!

Another passenger rushes in. An attractive female — looks like she could be my species — and she's coming my way. Best to remove my vow ring. I place it in my pocket, then stand so she can pass into the pod. She brushes against me, and I smell pleasant, exotic scents. She surprises me when she sits in the seat closest to me.

A holographic image appears. "This is Commander Duckworth. I'll be the shuttle pilot for your flight," he says in his south-planet accent. "Everything's automated, so I'm kinda redundant, but I'll be around to make sure everything's shipshape. Sun bursts and meteor showers are expected to be at a minimum, so we'll probably arrive ahead of schedule. With these new hyperdrive deluxe engines, we'll be arriving at your destination before we leave. Have a good flight, y'all."

The attendant gives us our warnings. "Remember to turn off all replicators, lasers, and the new holo games that fire back. We don't want to interfere with the automated instruments and go kaboom!"

A few chortle, but it's always the same thing. "In the event of an emergency, exit in an orderly fashion into the escape pod and insert the breathing tube that drops out of the pod ceiling all the way down your breathing hole. For creatures that have more than one, use the adjustable stoppers. Remember to properly insert the waste tube that pops up from the floor."

That last one — a new feature — has been sorely overlooked in the past.

As usual, no one is listening.

After the attendants sing their little departure song — yes, it's *that* shuttle service — the pod shell rises from the floor to encapsulate us for the long journey. I notice my pod-mate has raised the appendage rest between us, and she's smiling at me with her pointy even teeth. I have a feeling that I might just get lucky this trip.

◊

As the pods close, the passenger across the aisle nudges his companion. They glance across at the reptilian male with the slicked-down hair and the smiling, pointy-toothed female. "Did you know that those females devour anyone they mate with after copulation?"

———-•••••-——-

Ed Radwanski (aka **Luke Walters**) developed a passion for writing short stories after he won first prize in a 6th grade short story competition. He continued writing short stories throughout his lifetime, filling numerous notebooks, but work and raising a family took priority over publishing them. Now in retirement in Arizona, he's published several short stories online, a paperback collection entitled *Tales of Africa and Other Short Stories* (available on Amazon), and a novel entitled *Kill Me Quick* on Kindle Vella. Another collection of short stories — *Working It* — is scheduled for publication in December 2024. In his spare time, Ed is busy producing videos for his YouTube channel "Ed's Cycling with Coyotes," repairing old bicycles to donate to charity, and shepherding his backyard feral cat, who hasn't decided yet whether he's an indoor cat or an outdoor cat.

MINUS

Kathy Steinemann

BENJAMIN CARLISLE winced. "Egad!" *Minus-ten is too young.*

The middle-aged woman reclining in the chaise gnawed on her lip and twirled her parasol. "Do I really look so horrible?"

"Oh no, not at all. I had my finger over the lens. Stupid mistake. I apologize." He pushed his bifocals to the bridge of his nose and held a photo at arm's length. *The camera should have been calibrated for minus-five.*

A rueful smile covered his irritation. He crumpled the photo and threw it into the parlor fireplace. "Mrs. Pemberton, would you mind posing just once more? Here, have another sip of my special tea while I tinker with the f-stop."

"If you wish, I can send my liveryman back to the stable with the carriage — as long as you are willing to escort me home."

"Although I would enjoy the delightful company, madam, I have another client in thirty minutes. My messenger service can deliver your portrait tomorrow."

"You are such a talented inventor, Mr. Carlisle. Instant portraits — and in color!"

"My next invention will be a horseless carriage."

She harrumphed. "Then what will happen to all the horses, and liveries, and carriages?"

"The world will adapt." He adjusted the dial to minus-five and squinted as he peered through the viewfinder. "On three. Repeat after me. One ..."

Agatha raised her tweezed eyebrows. "One."

"Two ..."

She fluffed the frill at her neck. "Two."

"Three ..."

Her aloof expression transformed into a come-hither smile. "Three." She blinked in the intense brilliance of the flash.

Benjamin nodded. "That should be a winner."

He reviewed the still-moist likeness. "Excellent. I will frame this when my next sitting is finished."

"May I see it? Please?"

"You were informed of the conditions. No peeking. Satisfaction guaranteed."

Silently, she proffered her hand, nodded, and left the room.

He pressed the brown button to eject the photo. *Minus-five. Yes, five years younger makes her look good — but not so good that anyone would suspect.* He pressed the green button to make her age regression permanent.

◊

Mrs. Pemberton slept well that night, and in the morning she felt energized — better than she had in months. When the doorbell chimed, she hastened to the door and took receipt of the package. Now she would have a world-renowned Carlisle photograph. With trembling fingers, she peeled off the wrapping. She smiled. What an excellent portrait. The brown spots that had crept into her complexion over recent years were gone. Even the tiny crinkles at the edges of her eyes had disappeared.

Her husband barely moved his mutton chops behind his newspaper when she entered the parlor. He mumbled around the stem of his pipe, "Are you happy with the portrait, dear?"

"Yes! It makes me look so beautiful and young."

Mr. Pemberton glanced at the picture, then at her. His pipe dropped from his lips to his lap. "My dear, you appear especially fetching this morning." He stood and pulled her toward him. "Shall we go upstairs?"

"But, James, Saturday is still two days away."

He kissed her, passionately, and led her to their bedchamber.

◊

Benjamin scrutinized his invention. Two decades of lonely dedication, and now it was almost perfect. A twist of the dial, and the resulting photo appeared younger. A push of the green button, and the subject became the same age as his or her likeness. Benjamin's molecular-sized automatons, *nanomotes*, he called them, synchronized with his camera settings and performed their chores with speed and perfection.

He paced, his slippers slapping against his heels. *Is it time to tell the world, or shall I keep it a secret?* He gazed at his reflection in the mirror above the mantel. *One final test. I shall regress to just before I needed these blasted bifocals.*

Benjamin returned to the camera.

Spectacles off. Calibration minus-five. Done. He repositioned the tripod. Adjusted the angle. *F-stop ready. Chemical compartment full.* He recapped the bottles of highly combustible liquids. When satisfied that everything was properly prepared, he sipped from the nanomote-laced tea in his cup and triggered the remote shutter release.

The flash flared. Benjamin groped for his spectacles. His bushy eyebrows knit together in a frown. *Bollocks! I moved the dial too far.*

As he reached to correct the error, he bumped the tripod with his knee. His attempt to grab the camera was unsuccessful. It plummeted to the floor and splashed chemicals into the fireplace. Exploding fingers of flame clawed the curtains and set them ablaze.

He ran for water. When he returned to the parlor, the blaze had already spread to walls and furniture. Acrid smoke burned his eyes and filled his lungs. Choking, he fled to the front door, dashed outside, and watched the tongues of orange as they lapped at his house, his invention, his entire life's work.

He disappeared into the billowing blackness, stomping at sparks in the dry grass and searching for anything he could salvage.

Within minutes, neighbors noticed the inferno and formed a bucket brigade.

◊

After the last bucket of water had been emptied, everyone stood around the charred remains, sooty and breathless in the haze of steam and smoke, wondering what had become of Benjamin.

In a bizarre turn of events, nobody could determine the identity of the baby they discovered crawling in his front yard.

NEWTON'S SECOND LAW

-—-•◊•-—-

Kathy Steinemann

A TEAR TRICKLED from Muriel's chin into the cleavage peeking through her ultra-transparent pink negligee. She squared her jaw and swiped at the controls of her holovid transmitter.

The tired face of her friend Suzanne appeared, disheveled hair partially obscuring her eyes. "Muriel? What are you doing up so late? You look worried."

Muriel's reply was a quiet whisper in the dimly lit honeymoon suite. "I just need someone to talk to."

"Why are you being so quiet? What's the matter?"

She blew her nose. "It's Jovi."

"Is he —"

"He's in the bedroom. Sleeping. That's why I'm whispering."

"I thought he was on Mars."

"Yeah."

Suzanne blinked several times. "Either you're not making any sense, or I'm still asleep. Are you calling from Mars?"

Muriel dabbed at her mascara. "No. Jovi proposed. On his way back to Earth."

Suzanne squealed. "I'm *so* envious. Don't keep me in suspense. Tell me all the dirty details — and don't you dare leave *anything* out."

Muriel twisted a lock of hair in her fingers.

Suzanne's eyes grew larger. "No ... Don't tell me you turned him down!"

"Uh-uh."

Suzanne leaned forward until her face filled the entire view-field. "Then you should be happy. You're getting married to your childhood sweetheart."

"The wedding was this morning on the Ophanim shuttle. Just a quick ceremony with a justice of the peace. We booked this elaborate honeymoon suite, but ..."

"But what? Out with it."

"As soon as we touched down, Jovi collapsed."

"Oh no! Is he all right?"

"Yeah. He will be."

Suzanne shook her head. "C'mon girl. You've got me all confused. Spill."

Muriel blushed. "We didn't allow for a crucial fact. The gravity on Mars is only a third of Earth's. *Jovi* can hardly stand — never mind anything else."

QUID PRO QUO

Kathy Steinemann

THE BLUE BLOUSE. *That's what I'll wear to work tomorr —*
What was that?

Melodie frowned. She was sure she had seen a movement
in the corner of the closet. Her breath caught in her throat. *A*
mouse?

She hated mice almost as much as she dreaded the dark.

A shudder crept down her spine, and her trembling fingers
pushed a few hangers across the rod. She stared at the floor
between her umbrella and shoe rack. There. Something only
half visible, iridescent, twinkling into view and disappearing,
only to reappear a moment later. Her wondering scrutiny
followed its translucent shimmer from the floor up ... up ... to a
head squished against the ceiling.

The being shielded its brow to block the glare. Its large
eyes, set in recessed sockets, seemed to be pleading with her.
Melodie recoiled and forced the door closed. A voice whispered
in her head. *"Please do not fear."*

Her heart thumped against her ribs. She stumbled
backward. Her temples pounded, and the room swam around
her.

◊

As Melodie fought her way out of silent darkness, she sensed the voice again. The voice! It spoke to her consciousness — a soft whisper in her thoughts.

Her brain responded as though she had been a telepath all her life. *What are you? What did you do to me?*

"Me visitor from other planet. Broken ship. Need help."

Why me? I'm not a scientist or a computer technician.

"But knowledge you have."

She tiptoed closer and edged the door open. From an angular skull with silver peaks and shadowed valleys, large intelligent orbs inspected her. Its form no longer flickered, and although it towered over her by at least a foot, its slender humanoid form looked unimposing, with two arms and legs, and a compassionate face.

Its clothing changed color when it moved, a chameleon camouflage that made it almost invisible.

Her trepidation dissolved as she peered into its violet-blue eyes. *My name's Melodie. What's yours?*

"Xzaarin is what my kind call me."

How do you know English?

"Learning now ... from Melodie's mind and memories." Its tapered fingers reached toward her.

Mesmerized by its gaze, she felt no apprehension as its warm palms pressed against her temples.

Her consciousness filled with inaudible stroboscopic images. An ovoid spacecraft streaking through the atmosphere. Some kind of navigation system failure. A bumpy landing. Xzaarin traveling on foot for two days to reach Melodie's cabin on the edge of the woods. Xzaarin slipping into the warmth of her house while she was at work, then hiding in the closet when he heard her drive into the yard.

How long had the encounter lasted? She couldn't tell, but the influx of information made her dizzy. Endorphins pumped to her extremities. Twitches of ecstasy overwhelmed her. Her face burned with embarrassment, and a shudder shook her from toes to neck.

He stepped back a pace. *"You cannot withstand much more, but I think I gave you enough to understand my predicament."*

Her thoughts drifted — lethargic, drunk. Her body continued to pulse. *Uh huh ...* She blinked multiple times and then tried to focus on anything except the sensations sweeping through her. *How come you sound different? Ha ha. Sound different. What a joke.*

"It was a two-way exchange, a quid pro quo, as you humans say. Your language has many strange formations, but it is colorful and not too difficult to learn."

She touched his arm. *Thank you. My mind is full. I feel like Einstein or Tesla.*

Xzaarin grinned. *"Not good. Those scientists are dead."*

Melodie returned his grin. *That's something my mom might say if ...*

"You have a secret wish?"

She blushed. *I —*

"Do not fear. I did not explore the deepest parts of your subconscious. However, I was aware of a strong desire on the periphery of my probe."

She smiled. *You can look or listen or probe or whatever it is you do.* She pulled his palms to her forehead, eagerly anticipating the rush to follow ...

"Ah, yes. I see. You are an anomaly, unlike most of your race."

Her entire being vibrated with a euphoric sensation she had never before experienced as she realized what she should do next.

Melodie took a few seconds to calm her breathing and compose herself. Then she grasped Xzaarin's hand and led him to her laptop. His fingers tapped the keys in a rapid-fire salvo. A dim, bluish glow enveloped him. He stopped, palms flat on the keyboard. Page after page from the internet raced over the screen in an unreadable blur. Lines of light flowed from the wireless router to surround him in a whirlwind of sparkling specks and colors.

She watched, entranced, as Xzaarin faded and then became solid once more. Somehow, her newfound insight understood that he was absorbing the knowledge of the net.

After several minutes, he nodded. *"Now I know where to find what I need, and I understand your wish."*

◊

Melodie woke in her dark bedroom. She squinted as she studied her surroundings. The computer sat idle on her desk. *Was I dreaming?* She rolled out of bed and padded across the carpet to the window. A flash of vibrant brilliance streaked from the treetops to the star-studded sky beyond.

"No you were not dreaming. Good-bye, Melodie. Much gratitude for your assistance. I found the components I required in a warehouse near your cabin. They will do until I get home and replace them with the correct parts. I believe you would refer to this as a bubblegum repair. Oh ... I also found out how to get 10,000 new Twitter followers at a low, low price."

She chuckled as she waved at the disappearing point of light. *Good-bye, Xzaar —*

Her hand flew to her mouth. Her eyes widened. *My laugh. I heard it.* Her breath caught in her throat. For the first time since her surgery for a brain tumor six years ago, she could hear the muted clink of the heat registers and the whisper of her breathing.

"Thank you, Xzaarin," she murmured, with a smile he might have seen from a million miles away, "I think I'll call my mom."

SANITATION PROTOCOLS

Kathy Steinemann

A) Food

1. All personnel must observe strict sanitation protocols, especially around the young and the elderly. Said groups are at highest risk for illness from parasitic infections in unsterilized food and surroundings.

2. Cleanse all appendages frequently, especially those used for consuming nourishment.

3. Decontaminate your bodies and clothing in sterilization locks before changing locations.

B) Equipment

1. Once daily, dismantle and disinfect all machinery. Use only approved cleaning products listed in Appendix A, mixed as per instructions. Do not over-dilute.

2. Perform visual checks of all components for residue. Parasites are small, and may be missed if you do not practice due diligence. Employ probes to inspect hidden areas.

3. If all sterilization attempts fail, report infected equipment to your section commander. Personnel will then place said equipment on the trash transport and jettison it into the sun, along with any Earthlings still attached.

WINDOW WASHERS

Kathy Steinemann

BILLY'S PLAINTIVE VOICE shrieked from the living room, "Daddy, Daddy, help!"

Kaleb raced toward his son, who dangled out the window, a single peanut-buttery hand clinging to the ledge four stories above the noisy traffic below.

Kaleb gripped Billy's elbow, grabbing more sleeve than arm. "I've got you." His tenuous hold began to slip. He gritted his teeth. His breath came in short bursts as a surge of adrenaline seized him. "Hold still."

Billy's eyes flooded with tears.

A window washer in a neon-blue superhero outfit swung into view and clutched the boy by the waist. "I've got him." The man released Billy into his father's arms. "Here you go, sir."

Another window washer, clad in a cat costume, appeared from above their heads.

Kaleb squeezed his son to his chest. "Billy Galloway, how many times have I told you to keep the window closed when you're flying paper airplanes in the living room?" His misty gaze drifted to Billy's Good Samaritan. "Thank you so much, sir."

"IsoZap's the name. Window washing's my game." One arm bent in a salute to Billy. Then he thrust out his chest, emphasizing the fake muscles and bright yellow comet on his uniform, before he thumped Mr. Galloway on the shoulder. "Now I have to return to GyroKat." He grinned. "The pretty kitty doesn't do a proper job unless I give her lots of help and supervision."

Billy sobbed, and his chin trembled. "I'm sorry, Daddy."

"It's okay. The important thing is you're safe."

Billy's saucer-eyed gawp shifted to IsoZap. "Daddy, is it really *him*?"

"I guess it must be. Lucky he was here to save you, right?"

"Yeah." He watched IsoZap's clumsy movements and studied the fake fur of GyroKat's black costume with its flapping silver cape. "Na, they aren't real superheroes. Can I go play some more?" Without waiting for a reply, he scurried into the kitchen to make another airplane.

Kaleb watched the window washers as they descended out of sight. *Management must have hired a new maintenance company. I'm glad they were here when we needed help.* He swatted at a mosquito. "Damn blood-sucking little vampires."

◊

That afternoon in a different part of the city, a man with a bushy beard entered the director's office on the top floor of The Extraterrestrial Search Project building. He aimed his .45 at Billy's mother, Elvina Galloway. She raised her hands and edged toward the security buzzer hidden under the carpet.

A svelte woman in a cat costume and her male partner in neon-blue crashed through the skylight. They knocked the man over. The woman kicked his weapon away. The male superhero seized the trespasser and zip-tied his wrists.

Mrs. Galloway collapsed into her chair, slack-jawed and quivering, staring at the garb of television superheroes, IsoZap and GyroKat.

GyroKat stood over the intruder in victorious stance. "Perhaps you should contact 911, ma'am."

Elvina stared at the bearded man for one rasping breath, then replied, "Thank you for being here when I needed help." With trembling fingers, she picked up the phone.

◊

IsoZap and GyroKat sat opposite each other at her tiny dinette table.

He examined what appeared to be a large mosquito and gave his partner a playful nudge. "Lucky we were there on surveillance when Billy went over the edge."

She inspected the mosquito. "Yes. When I think of what might have happened ... Did the bot find anything in the apartment?"

"No, Elvina's too paranoid to take confidential material home." He cocked his head. "She didn't notice when I switched flash drives during the supposed robbery attempt. Operative X0321 said our fake thief escaped phony police custody according to plan. Elvina was shaken, but she'll be okay."

GyroKat spooned more sugar into her coffee. "Your sleight of hand never ceases to amaze me. Elvina would be even more shaken if she knew the truth about Kaleb. I'll be glad when we can get rid of these stupid costumes. Window washers dressed up as superheroes? It's fine for the children's hospital, but we're adults, for Pete's sake."

◊

Elvina sank into the softness of the sofa and propped her feet on an ottoman as she yelled toward the kitchen. "Thanks, Kal. Supper was delicious." She pulled a pile of printouts from her briefcase. "Did you have any luck yet tracking down your biological parents?"

Kaleb padded across the carpet and kissed the top of her head. "You're welcome, and no. Bio-Lokato hasn't produced any results. I'll check again in the morning. I'm sorry your day was so hectic."

"Thanks." She exhaled a protracted sigh.

"Are you all right? You seem preoccupied."

"We're working on an important project at ESP. Once the data is verified, I'll be able to relax." She pressed the power button on the TV remote.

Kaleb shuffled away and tucked Billy in, his thoughts of a romantic evening relegated to the distant recesses of his mind. Elvina became an ice queen whenever things got hectic at work.

He climbed into their king-size bed with the cold silk sheets, and was still awake when Elvina eventually slipped under the covers and turned her back to him.

◊

With morning came the usual disorganized rush of little-boy shenanigans and appeals to finish just one more video game before kindergarten. Kaleb said no and walked Billy to the school-bus stop after breakfast.

The odors of auto fumes and burnt hash-browns from a nearby restaurant permeated the air. Kaleb shivered in the brisk spring breeze as he attempted to concentrate on his son's non-stop monologue about *Mario Kart 22.* However, his thoughts drifted.

He frowned during the walk home. This stay-at-home-dad routine had turned out to be more difficult than expected. Kaleb had given up a prestigious position in a successful financial firm to work as a freelance accountant — while Elvina earned all the big bucks, and hobnobbed with famous scientists and statesmen. He loved his son, but some days he resented the new family structure.

Added to the home dynamics was the relationship with his adoptive parents. Facetime sessions from Auckland weren't the same as real visits, and lately the sessions had seemed strained. His folks said they were supportive of his search for his blood relatives, but he wondered if their encouragement was mere empty words.

◊

The tomb-silent apartment was too quiet. He turned on the stereo, fired up his laptop, and reached for his favorite coffee mug — the mug Billy had made him for Christmas. *Crap. I don't remember finishing this.* He ambled to the kitchen and waited for a fresh pot to brew. *Will I ever find my parents? I deserve to know who they are, and Billy deserves to know all of his grandparents.*

The final burbles of the coffee maker jolted him back to reality. Seven teaspoons of sugar in a steaming mug of medium-roast Sumatra blend. *Perfect.*

He returned to the study and checked the Bio-Lokato database to see if there were any search results for his biological family.

Nothing.

Leaning back in his chair, he interlaced his fingers behind his neck and glowered at the stack of receipts and papers on his desk. *The accounting files can wait. I'm going to keep looking.*

◊

Elvina keyed a security code into her encrypted transmitter. "This is Beta."

"Please hold."

She sighed, and fingered the flash drive in her pocket.

"Do you have it?"

"Yes, Madam President. All the proof we need. Nobody will ever doubt The Extraterrestrial Search Project again. What happens next?" She listened to her instructions and nodded. "Yes, ma'am. I'll load the data onto my computer as soon as we finish this conversation."

After a respectful farewell to her Commander in Chief, Elvina disconnected. She slid the flash drive into a vacant slot and waited for it to load.

Either it was empty or —

Icons disappeared. The computer display filled with strange glyphs and scrolling alphanumeric characters. She removed the drive and pushed the power switch. Nothing happened. She tried to disengage the wireless connection. The computer wouldn't respond.

She dialed IT. Busy signal. Three tries later, she was able to get through.

IT informed her that a virus had already infiltrated every system in the building, and was in the process of contaminating The ESP grid.

She disconnected. Dialed an emergency number.

Several network error messages answered her repeated attempts to phone out.

Finally, she was able to connect. "This is Beta. I think they've discovered we're onto them."

"Hold on. ... Wait a minute. ... A worm is propagating to every computer and electronic device connected via wireless or the net. I don't think we can prevent it from infecting every unprotected system on Earth."

Elvina slumped over her desk — and cried.

◊

Kaleb greeted Elvina at the door. "Couldn't do much work this afternoon. The internet is down, and a virus wiped out a bunch of my files. I asked your mom to babysit Billy at her place, and I made an extra-special supper. I thought maybe you and I ..."

Elvina scrutinized the candlelit place settings. "I'm sorry I've been such a witch lately. I'm working on a big project, something really important. But some damn hacker stole several gigabytes of confidential information, and we've got computer problems, and IT is sweeping for bugs, and ... I guess I have an unexpected vacation."

He gulped. His voice lowered to a throaty whisper. "It's too bad about the breach, but that could be an advantage for us, right? Maybe we'll get some quality time alone now."

◊

GyroKat dumped a generous helping of sugar into her cup. "I wonder what Elvina intended to do with this flash drive."

IsoZap smirked. "Just the kind of stupid remark I'd expect from a cat who can't land on her feet. We caught the purrrrrr-petrator."

She smoothed her whiskers. "Hey! That's my line."

IsoZap peeled off his hood. "Operatives X0618 and X0432 located the guy who put this data together — Nigel Schnuffler. They did a selective memory wipe, and Schnuffler seems to have forgotten about us. We have to maintain surveillance, though, just in case. That's your job, super-kitty."

GyroKat scowled. "Let's get serious. The worm wiped out every incriminating photo, video, and information file faster than IsoZap racing to the washroom with a case of the trots."

His cheeks dimpled. "Okay, okay. Enough with the inane humor. I thought we were getting serious. Thanks to our efforts, everyone's interests have been protected."

Their contented smiles and raised mugs celebrated a mission accomplished.

GyroKat contemplated her coffee. "We still don't know how Schnuffler found out about us." She sipped. Wrinkled her nose. Added several more teaspoons of sugar. "If Elvina hadn't been so anal about keeping the data on her person, we would have finished weeks ago. I'm glad this is over."

He shrugged. "I'll miss the intrigue. I enjoyed this assignment."

"You're not the superhero who gets ogled and whistled at." Her cellphone rang with a series of soft bleeps. "Operative X0392 speaking. ... Yes, sir, we're ready to begin the final phase. ... Yes, sir." She disconnected the call and activated the holovid.

They reviewed 3-D images through moist eyes.

Smiling faces waving at the holorecorder. A city reduced to cinders and bones. Before and after views of a faraway planet: continents and oceans that had transformed into ashes and steam. Thousands of inanimate bodies in translucent tubes, stacked in rows and columns inside a cylindrical space.

IsoZap sighed. "We'll have to tell Kaleb someday that his family is dead. It's not fair to let him keep looking for them."

After their faces had dried, they reviewed the flash drive they stole from Elvina.

The first video showed people materializing in a forest clearing: shifting, shimmering shapes that became solid as they walked out of camera view.

Another recording contained time-lapse surveillance of two houses, filmed as some of the same people entered and left the premises.

A third was a collage of scenes showing the people intermingling, unnoticed, among those with whom they worked.

The recording ended with audio superimposed over a static photo of the forest clearing. *"They're everywhere. They could be teaching our kids, driving our taxis, flying our planes. There's no way to tell who they are or what they want. The alien invasion has begun. Are we going to let them take over our planet? Or are we going to defend ourselves?"*

GyroKat's cellphone rang with the initial bars from "Hail to the Chief". She answered before it completed its first ring cycle. "Yes, Madam President. ... Yes. ... I agree. ... Our covers are intact, and we transferred all settlers to different safehouses. ... Yes, ma'am. ... Thank you, ma'am. ... You, too."

She disconnected, and pulled off her cape.

IsoZap raised his eyebrows. "Do you intend to share, or are you planning to keep it a secret?"

"The final psychological results confirm that humans wouldn't accept us without overt resistance. And the President intends to tell Kaleb he's not from Earth."

"That was it?"

"Oh, you want the long version." GyroKat grinned. "Billy's birth and excellent health proves our races are compatible. She has given approval to transport all our remaining survivors to the surface so that we can integrate them into Earth society. Thanks to those of us who have assumed the reins of power, this planet will never face the same kind of particle accelerator miscalculation that almost destroyed us."

◊

Elvina smiled. "Another excellent supper, hon."

Her encrypted cellphone rang. She answered. "Is something wrong?" After listening for a few seconds, she pinched her lips and handed the phone to Kaleb. "It's the President's office. She wants to speak to you."

Elvina sat on the carpet next to the sofa and studied her toenails as she listened to Kaleb's halting conversation, which was punctuated by an occasional "Yes, Madam President" or "No, Madam President." He scratched his chin. Got up and paced around the room. Sat down again. Partway through the conversation his face blanched, and he stuttered a few words Elvina couldn't understand.

After several minutes, he ended the call and leaned forward to kiss Elvina's head.

She gazed up. "What was that all about?"

"Um ... I've been offered an interesting job that I can work around Billy's school schedule. I can't talk about it. Private and confidential."

She smiled with an indecipherable gleam in her eyes. "I'll make supper tomorrow night."

SQUARE-FARE

-—-•◊••—-

Kathy Steinemann

NEIL WRINKLED his nose as he chewed on the rubbery omelet his wife had prepared for breakfast. "Where'd you buy the egg substitute?"

Charlene shrugged. "Mauer-Mart. It was on sale."

"No more cheap stuff. I want Square-Fare eggs from now on."

"Square-Fare?"

"Yeah. You know — the new ones they're talking about on TV."

Neil stood and cleared his throat, gesturing while he mimicked the commercial. "Square-Fare eggs fit into square trays, optimizing shelf space in stores and kitchens. A shelf life three times longer than chicken eggs. Our superior product requires no refrigeration. Delicious and nutritious. Flavor-Faktor guaranteed. Healthy orange yolks and zero cholesterol. Square-Fare — worth the tiny extra you pay."

"Fine. Whatever. I'll try to save money by skimping on something else."

◊

Neil and Charlene — and millions of people around the world — had switched to Square-Fare by March. Square-Fare

144

produced "the best eggs" manufactured by "efficient machines" that spat nanocyte-rich blobs into square molds and conveyed them into a finishing chamber. There, the shells hardened, and depleted nanocytes dropped through the mesh below for recharging.

By the following year, most poultry farms had culled their flocks and bought Square-Fare franchises.

And Square-Fare continued to fine-tune their formula.

◊

Neil wrinkled his nose as he chewed on the rubbery omelet Charlene had made for lunch. "Where'd you buy the egg substitute?"

She frowned. "It's Square-Fare. I always get Square-Fare."

"Why does this crap taste like an old tire, then?"

"I didn't do anything different. Same recipe, same cooking time."

He shoved his plate away. "This is revolting. Let's order pizza."

◊

Neil and Charlene — and millions of people around the globe — e-mailed and telephoned Square-Fare's head office.

Square-Fare responded with a publicity campaign headed by a mascot in a chicken costume. "We made a slight change to the recipe," he clucked, "but we'll restore the original Flavor-Faktor formula."

Meanwhile, Square-Fare continued to use substandard ingredients in an attempt to increase profits.

◊

Neil smiled. "Excellent omelet, sweetheart."

"Not as excellent as my news."

"You don't mean —"

"Yes. I'm expecting! We're going to be parents."

Neil pulled Charlene into his arms and gave her a resounding kiss.

◊

Charlene — and thousands of Square-Fare female consumers around the world — became pregnant. Sadly, they all required emergency Caesarean sections to deliver babies with square heads that couldn't squeeze through round spaces. The researchers at Square-Fare hadn't counted on nanocytes infiltrating the food chain.

Square-Fare settled the lawsuits.

Then they reorganized, reformulated, and retooled.

◊

Neil glanced up from his news vid. "Good omelet, sweetheart."

Charlene replied, "Bwawk bwawk bwawk."

Square-Fare filed for bankruptcy.

STILL HERE

-—-•◊•-—-

Kathy Steinemann

CHARMAINE LEETO disappeared from the transmission unit of the transporter but didn't reappear as expected on the receiving platform three meters away.

The control room exploded with curses, chaotic activity, and speculation.

"What happened?"

"We need to get her back."

"Double-check the settings."

Daniel Odesta bellowed orders to fellow scientists, who poked panels, twisted dials, and rechecked calibrations. Then he hunched over his console, with his head in his hands.

Herman, his primary assistant, patted Daniel's shoulder. "Don't worry. We'll find her."

"How? This project is Charmaine's *baby*. We set everything according to her parameters, and nobody knows how to operate the transporter as efficiently as she does."

"Yeah, she probably made a mistake. It could take hours or even days to track down the error."

Daniel frowned. "She doesn't make mistakes. Don't speak ill of the —" *No, I can't think that way. Charmaine, sweetie, I know you're still here ... somewhere.*

Charmaine Leeto floated, atoms adrift, in a shimmering space devoid of smell and touch.

Her fogginess cleared. *Damn. What went wrong? I feel so strange — simultaneously everywhere and nowhere. Is this how the chimps felt? Couldn't be. They went through almost instantaneously. God, what have I done?*

An iridescent whirlwind swirled around her. *I wish I had a camera to record this.*

The outlines of familiar equipment and faces materialized. Even as she spoke, she realized nobody would hear, but she tried anyway. *Daniel, I'm still here, honey. I'm still here.* She reached toward him with fingertips that floated somewhere in the space-time continuum, knowing he wouldn't feel her touch. However, her need for human contact overwhelmed the detached scientist in her.

Her sadness would have manifested as tears if she'd had a body.

I'm still here.

A second presence percolated into her awareness, a presence with confused, incoherent thoughts: jumbled impressions of warmth and light mixed with darkness and sound and feeling. The vague visions and shapes made no sense to her. She tried to probe for a mental connection, a clue, anything that would help her understand. She detected fear. Was the fear hers? Or that of the entity?

◊

Daniel and Herman dashed from station to station, conferring with console operators, and checking figures. They couldn't find a reason for the anomaly. Minutes passed — minutes that crawled as though they were hours.

Daniel massaged the headache between his eyebrows as he dropped into his chair. "Seven chimpanzees went through, over and over, without any problems. They're all normal and healthy. Charmaine never would have insisted on being the first person through, otherwise. She's cautious, and she always pays scrupulous attention to protocol." He pointed to the settings. "Look, everything's correct. The safety measures should have worked."

Herman whispered from behind his hand, "I'm sorry. I know that you two —"

"What?"

"C'mon, we've all seen the way you look at each other. We're trained observers. Did you really think you could hide it?"

Daniel chewed on his lower lip. They had been so careful not to reveal —

Careful. That's it! The creases on his brow relaxed, and he smiled. Without a word, he elbowed Herman aside and entered something into the main console.

A swirling, iridescent pattern formed on the receiving platform.

Everyone in the room clapped and applauded when Charmaine reappeared, confusion evident in her expression.

Daniel shrugged. *What the hell. Everyone knows now.* He embraced her and gave her a passionate kiss. "Thank God, you're back!"

She returned the kiss, wide-eyed, then pulled away. "Daniel!"

"It's okay. The cat's out of the bag."

She gulped as she looked around the lab. "How long was I gone?"

"Just a few minutes. There was a slight error in the settings."

"No way. I triple-checked everything."

"On a hunch, I overrode the system and changed something. Two persons —"

"Two?"

He grinned and kissed her again. "We weren't careful enough. I think we're about to become parents."

COMPETING FOR KALLISTA

-·——·◊··——·-

Kathy Steinemann

"OUCH!" KALLISTA SLID her bouquet of roses into a vase and dabbed at the pinprick of blood on her fingertip. "Who sent these, vinDara?"

The butler-bot responded in a singsong tenor. "There was no note, Ms. Kallista."

Kallista sighed. *Which of my husbands was it this time?*

She repositioned stems, careful to avoid another stab, then pulled a sprig of baby's breath from the bouquet and poked it behind her ear. She flashed back to last night's conjugal visit: tender hands stroking baby's breath from her lips to her breasts, down to her ankles, and back up again. She shivered with delight, and a smile ghosted her lips as she set the vase aside and strolled to the front door.

Kallista stared at her coat-hook. Three favorite scarves. Which should she pick today? She grimaced. Unlike her scarves, she never got to pick which husband would share her nights. Three good-bye kisses every morning. Three recliners in the living room. Three men who competed to be the dominant spouse.

She was tired of her husbands' secret bets and bargains to swap time with her, of not knowing who would come to her room at the end of the day.

Jon? Atlin? Wodge? Who would tonight's bed warmer be?

She had suggested the random scheme when they got married. The uncertainty titillated her at first. It seemed sexy and intriguing. Kinky. But she regretted the arrangement more every day. She was exhausted.

And now she was expected to go on a holiday with one of them. *Whoopee.*

Kallista stared at the ceiling and bit her lip.

It *was* her fault. She had chosen them from hundreds of suitors and twenty-four proposals.

Jon: efficient, handsome, abreast of world events and financial trends. His wit and suave manners had charmed her.

Atlin: athletic, self-confident, mischievous. Nobody could compete with his sense of humor.

Wodge: a bit of a nerd. No Prince Charming, but there was something about his smile. And she tingled when he touched her.

Kallista had done her civic duty. Nobody could fault her. In fact, she had won the *Model Citizen Medal* several times. However, sometimes she wished for the days when relationships were simpler — one person to come home to, to share your conversations and dreams, to hold your hand when you strolled on the boardwalk.

She had no time to brood at work. Always another project. Multiple employees calling "Kallista" whenever they ran into a programming glitch.

But at the end of the day, her ride home in the anti-grav tube was always fraught with uncertainty. Who would she sleep with tonight? Jon the cover hog? Atlin the snorer? Wodge the spooner?

Kallista hugged herself.

◊

Jon primped in front of the full-length mirror in his bedroom and checked his posterior profile in the mirror tiles on the opposite wall.

Perfect.

He rubbed his chin. Close shave. Exactly the way Kallista liked it. He nodded.

Today's meeting with Sandi Bonze, CEO of the International Space Syndicate, could propel his career forward faster than any of his previous ploys and hustles. His income would double. His increased prestige would be enough to make Kallista choose him as the father of her future children.

He'd sire smart girls who could lead companies, and assertive boys who would do anything to succeed.

If only he could get her to choose her plaid scarf today. He wanted to spend this vacation alone with her — minus Atlin or Wodge eavesdropping from the shadows.

Jon heaved an extended sigh.

◊

Atlin mopped the sweat off his forehead. Final set of seventy pushups. That would be enough for now.

Endorphins engulfed him in a wave of wellbeing that helped compensate for his frustration at being one of three husbands.

Would Kallista choose him if he won the Intercontinental Ironman Triathlon? He could be the progenitor of superior children. Progeny that would improve the human race. Supple girls who loved Yoga. Strong boys who excelled at sports.

But in the meantime, he was damned to this miserable sham of a marriage.

He pummeled his punching bag. If only he could get Kallista to choose her blue scarf. The triathlon was still months away, and he wanted to spend this vacation with her. Just her. No Jon or Wodge to muscle in on their time together.

Atlin gritted his teeth.

◊

Wodge hyperventilated.

Could a geek like him pull off this switcheroo? He'd been working on it for two interminable years.

He didn't have a hope in hell of outdoing Jon or Atlin when it came to business negotiations or brute strength. *Jon and Atlin. Ha! Arrogant jerks.* They despised nerds and tossed their weight around like the aggressive bullies they were. He was tired of playing Mr. Niceguy with men he detested.

Maybe his innovative sex-surrogate androids would gain him the recognition he craved. He had developed lightweight droids that compressed small enough to fit into a carry-on suitcase.

Nah. Even if his innovations did win awards and garner acknowledgement from the scientific community, Kallista might choose Jon or Atlin first.

Cold sweat formed on his brow. His hands shook. *Calm down. You can do this.*

He squeezed his eyes closed and willed his body to relax while he imagined scenes of a meadow filled with baby's breath, flitting songbirds, and pleasant aromas. And there, floating on a cloud of white flowers, Kallista. His goddess. The mother of his future children. They'd have little girls with dancing ringlets and handsome boys with freckles.

Ahhhhh, yes. Much better.

Wodge tiptoed into the kitchen and accessed vinDara's programming module. He inserted a miniscule chip with program modifications, and rebooted the butler-bot.

That should do it.

He smiled.

◊

A tap on Kallista's shoulder interrupted her musing.

Jon raised his blond eyebrows. His slender fingers stroked her scarves. "Picked one yet? I prefer the plaid."

She craned her neck back to appraise his slim Nordic features. "No. Why are you so interested?"

"Just wondering." He shrugged, and fastened a button on his immaculate tweed suit. "Whatever you do, don't choose the yellow one." He leaned down to kiss her on the forehead. "I have an important meeting in thirty minutes. Must run. Have a good day."

He disappeared out the door before she had a chance to protest about his abrupt departure.

She wiped the moist imprint from her brow.

Atlin appeared. "Tsk tsk. I heard that. What could be more important than you?" He tugged at her blue silk scarf. "Here. Why don't you wear this?"

"What's with all the interest in my scarves? I'll make my own choice, if that's all right with you!"

"Sorry. Didn't mean to —"

"Right. What's the latest bet?" She studied the twinkle in his brown eyes.

Atlin smirked and pulled her close for a hug. "Stay away from the yellow one, okay?"

His shirt reeked of perspiration. She murmured against his broad chest, "You really should have a shower after your workouts."

"Scientific research shows that women get turned on by the smell of a real man."

"And the scientists who did the research are probably all males with aquaphobia."

He laughed. "Whatever. Have a wonderful day, and don't work too hard. Those guys at starrNyx don't deserve you." He puffed a lock of hair away from her throat and nuzzled his lips into the tender spot where neck joins shoulder.

She squirmed. "Go. Get out of here. No shower, no sugar."

"Yes, ma'am." He saluted, patted her cheek, and left, whistling as he clicked the door shut.

Wodge entered the foyer. He wasn't tall like Jon or muscular and tanned like Atlin. Wodge was ... Wodge. He stood for a moment, eyes partially closed, an introspective expression on his face. Then he walked toward her. Kallista wondered whether his eyes would look blue or green.

Blue.

She squinted at him. "I suppose you want me to choose the yellow scarf."

He gazed away, and his smile wavered. She pursed her lips.

Wodge pulled all the scarves from the coat-hook and draped them around her neck. He drew her close, his breath caressing the stray hairs at her temple, and whispered, "You pick whatever scarf you want."

A shiver engulfed her, and a tiny gasp escaped her lips as she tried a witty comeback. "What? You don't want me to pick yours — the yellow one?"

He kissed her. A slow kiss that left her wanting more. "You look gorgeous, no matter what you're wearing. And even better stripped down to your bare skin. I love you, Kallie. I'd do anything for you."

He pulled away and strode toward the door.

Kallista folded her arms across her breasts. *What are you scoundrels up to this time?*

◊

Wodge was tired of the skewed gender ratio caused by population control and a preference for boy babies, a preference that had created a world with 2.67 times as many males as females. He was fed up with polygamy and attempting to sleep when he knew Kallista was with Jon or Atlin instead of him.

Every morning he went to work at Cyber-Surrogates Inc., sat at the console in his office, designed new android parts, and analyzed quality-control stats.

Then, every afternoon, he swapped places with his droid duplicate.

Wodge had designed his double in a decommissioned lab. While doppelgänger-Wodge toiled at Wodge's console, real-Wodge slipped away to putter on his private project.

However, his plans for today varied from the norm.

His heart fluttered like the wings of a trapped bat, and his breathing rasped in an uneven rhythm. He swallowed. *You can do this.*

He initiated his voice-simulator/phone-ID spoofer, selected the vinDara profile, and called Jon.

◊

Jon checked his call display. "Sandi, do you mind if I take this? It could be important."

Sandi Bonze uncrossed her long legs, revealing her lack of panties, and leaned back on the desk. "Don't take too long. My motor's running, and it needs a fuel injection."

Jon's sweaty hands almost lost their grip on his phone as he spoke. "Hey, vinDara. Did I win?"

"Good morning, Mr. Jon. Yes, Ms. Kallista chose the plaid scarf. AstroTravel has booked you the mountain-climbing trek you requested on Mount Huashan. She will meet you at 6 p.m. outside the Metropolis III Terminal. Your belongings are packed and ready to go."

Jon's eyes sparkled. "Fantastic!" He lowered his voice. "I have to run. In a meeting."

He smiled and turned to Sandi, stripping off his shirt and tie as he sauntered to her waiting arms. A man had needs. One night in three wasn't enough.

◊

Atlin's phone vibrated against his thigh. *vinDara. Finally.*

He yelled over the loud music to his Uber-Exo class. "Carry on with what you're doing while I take this call." He continued to ogle the bouncing boobs and firm butts while he cradled his phone against one ear.

"Good morning, Mr. Atlin. Ms. Kallista chose the blue scarf. You are the winner of your desired scuba-diving getaway to the Tongue of the Ocean. She will be waiting outside your fitness center at 6 p.m. She has already packed your suitcase."

Atlin tried to hide his enthusiasm from the class, but he was sure the growing bulge in his sweatpants would give him away. Sunlight glinted through the skylight and glanced off the blinding whiteness of his teeth, which were framed in a humongous smile.

Screw you, Jon and Wodge.

◊

Wodge rubbed his hands together. Another misdirected husband. First phase of the charade complete.

All three men had arranged to take the next two weeks off. Atlin and Jon hoped they would win the bet about which of Kallista's favorite scarves she would choose today. But her choice was irrelevant. Wodge's plan made *him* the real winner.

He secured his office door and opened the safe to reveal doppelgänger-Wodge, a convoluted mishmash of body parts squished into the confined space. He energized the droid, which unfurled like a Chinese tea flower as it sprouted, expanded, and stretched toward the ceiling. "All systems active, sir."

Wodge stared at the android awaiting his commands. Medium height with ginger-brown hair, firm chin, and inquisitive eyes that seemed either blue or green, depending on the light conditions. The experience of seeing and hearing himself mirrored in the android always produced a heartbeat of surprise. "Your assignment for now is to interface with System X18-B and re-compute the performance specs for parts A389-E through A448-D. We've received reports of premature wear and failure."

"Yes, sir."

"Keep the door locked, and notify me immediately via uplink if anything ... Never mind. Keep your uplink connection open."

"Understood, sir."

Wodge slipped away to his secret lab.

◊

Kallista finished packing her suitcases. Which husband would accompany her on her two-week holiday? She stopped in mid-stride on her way to the kitchen and stroked the yellow scarf around her neck while she smiled an uncertain smile. *Wodge?*

She wanted to know for sure. Just once. No not once. Forever. She wanted stability; to know every who, when, and how of her marriage.

If only the world could return to old-fashioned norms. *Equal Opportunity Marriage. Right. Equal opportunity for men while women remain victims of a male-dominated government. Nothing has changed for centuries.*

But last night —

If only every night could be so perfect.

How many times had it been? Three? Four? She smiled. That kind of tired she could cope with.

However, tired was tired. She needed this break from her programming duties at starrNyx Solutions. If necessary, she could fake a headache whenever she wanted a night off from this ridiculous "second honeymoon."

Maybe I'll fake a headache every night. Hmm. Lots of time before we have to leave. I think I'll relax with a good book and fetch my passport from the safe later.

◊

Wodge entered his password into the lab's security panel. The door swished open.

Kallista, will you ever love me as much as I love you? He blinked and shook his head. *Get a grip.*

The lights activated as he walked in.

A couple of minor adjustments remained on the Kallista android. She was breathtaking in her perfection. Oak-auburn hair softly framed her face. Exactly the right amount of blush bloomed on her fair cheeks. A tiny scar on her right forearm hinted at a misadventure with a kitchen knife.

After synching the droid's neural net, he engaged her cognitive functions.

Her copper-brown eyes fluttered open. "Wodge? Where am I?"

Damn! I hit the wrong button. "Shhhh. It's all right."

"Wodge! What —" She shrieked and tried to break free of her charging station.

His thumb shifted on the remote regulator. Her mouth stopped moving.

He disengaged her neural network, made the final adjustments, and touched her face with trembling fingers. *Yes. She's flawless, exactly like the first Kallista droid.* He stood, watching both androids, thoughts spinning so fast he felt dizzy. *This has to work. It has to.*

He skulked through stairs and deserted hallways back to his office, where he led doppelgänger-Wodge to the safe. The man-sized droid curled into its compact fetal position while Wodge stood guard. Once the blink of the red indicator confirmed that the safe was locked, he brought up the Kallista droids' encrypted data feeds on his vid-screen.

Perfect.

Soon they would travel to their designated locations. His extra programming would change the droids' memories just enough to accommodate his plan.

When he pressed the *Execute* button, Jon and Atlin would disappear, never to be found, sent to their deaths by Kallista doubles — who would self-destruct when their tasks were complete.

Authorities would search mountain and ocean for remains, but they wouldn't be overly alarmed when they couldn't find anything. Avalanches happened. Sharks attacked. It wouldn't be the first time people had gone missing without a trace. Why worry about two men when the planet already had too many?

And then, Kallista would be his.

Forever.

If he could go through with it. Was he really that cold and heartless?

He tugged on his bottom lip while he paced. Two weeks. He had two weeks to decide whether or not to enable the *Execute* sequence.

◊

Wodge removed his jacket. "Good evening, vinDara. Is everything ready?"

"Yes, sir. Flowers, champagne, and meal menus in the auto-chef."

"Where's Kallista?"

"She said she wasn't feeling well and went to bed with a book."

Wodge frowned. "Monitor all incoming calls and don't allow any interruptions."

"Yes, Mr. Wodge." vinDara stood at attention next to the door, closed his eyes, and interfaced with the communications system.

Wodge tiptoed across the plush carpet in Kallista's room to her silent form in the bed. Her eyes remained closed. A tentative touch of her forehead revealed no fever. He smiled a wistful smile, and whispered, "Poor sweetheart. She's exhausted." Then he pulled the duvet up to cover her bare shoulders.

A slight rustling to the right caught his attention.

His eyes widened.

He gawped in confusion.

His head twisted, alternating from the sleeping Kallista to the Kallista standing beside him.

Wodge inhaled. *Yes.* Something he could never replicate in a lab. A subtle, sweet fragrance that wasn't perfume or flowers. It was better — like a combination of nutmeg and lilies.

Pure Kallista.

But who was it coming from? The Kallista under the duvet? Or the Kallista next to his shoulder?

He stumbled back a step and cocked his head. Had one of his assassin-bots gone berserk?

The standing Kallista brought her fingers to his lips. "Wodge, it's really you. And you were willing to let me sleep? Your chivalry is part of why I adore you."

"But I don't under —"

"She's an android. I had her custom-made. I didn't know who I heard coming into the house just now, so I switched with her. Whenever it's not your turn, she takes my place."

"What ...?"

Kallista smiled. "If Jon or Atlin steals one of your nights, I leave to 'freshen up,' then send the android back in my place. They're so clueless they can't tell the difference. Smart asses."

He bit his lip. "I'm your favorite?"

"Yes. You always have been. You're not arrogant or overbearing, and you pay attention to my needs. Little notes under my pillow. Baby's breath. Making sure I'm satisfied when we make love."

Kallista wrapped her arms around his neck. "I'm going to ask Jon and Atlin for dissolutions. Equal Opportunity Marriage be damned. I've had it with being a Model Citizen." She kissed him. A slow kiss that left him wanting more.

But —

Wodge dropped onto the bed.

He reached for the regulator in his pocket and fingered it for several seconds. *The only thing that could be better than Jon and Atlin's disappearances will be the shocked look on their smug mugs when they realize they've been sleeping with sex surrogates designed by me.*

He drew his hand out of his pocket, grabbed Kallista's elbows, and pulled her onto the bed. "Come here. I intend to keep you busy all night, every night, for the next two weeks."

FLUXXATRON MALFUNCTION

-—-•◊•-—-

Kathy Steinemann

This story is a reprint from Kathy's book *Suppose: Drabbles, Flash Fiction, and Short Stories.*

◊

SAMANTHA FISCHER pointed to an underwater shadow off the starboard side of the boat. "I think that's a torpedo heading toward us."

Her boyfriend, Jamie, adjusted his binoculars. "Impossible. Where would a torpedo come from in this remote area of the islands?"

Samantha laughed. It was the kind of laugh her mother always made when Samantha did something stupid. "Not a man-made torpedo, doofus, a torpedo stingray. Look. It's dipping and swaying in the water like a ballerina."

A lone seagull circled above the boat. Its high-pitched call sounded like a warning: "Die. Die. Die."

The ray accelerated its approach. The boat lurched and stayed suspended on the crest of a wave as the ray passed beneath it. A buzz filled the air, and electricity arced from metal to metal. Sparks exploded into steaming jets of water. The boat listed.

Samantha's head hit something hard.

When she came to, the boat and Jamie were gone. The ray swam beneath her, holding her afloat near a lifejacket. She paddled away.

Struggling to keep from swallowing seawater, her eyes frantic, she watched the creature. Two green apertures next to its gill slits glowed like neon lights. She tried to don the lifejacket.

The creature moved closer. Nudged her.

She pushed at it with both hands. "Go away. Leave me alone." Its eyes blinked and widened. She gaped into their crystal depth. And stopped thrashing.

The water drew her down, down. Soon she was floating in a strange place, submerged in a rhythmic sound that might have been music or machinery. She closed her eyes to alleviate the dizziness caused by fluctuating pressure in her ears, and drifted in darkness, with patterns of flickering light lulling her into unconsciousness.

◊

The sweet sunshine of a sandy beach caressed her body. The rough tongue of a sable Burmese cat lapped the seaweed from her brow. She gazed into its yellow-green eyes and shuddered as she remembered the torpedo ray. A young boy shook her shoulder. "Hey, lady. You okay?"

She mumbled.

He moved closer. "What?"

"Where's Jamie?"

"There's only you, lady. If you're okay, I'll go get my dad and mom."

Samantha nodded, then closed out the world again.

A flock of seagulls swooped and drifted above her. Their cries echoed from the cliffs, becoming fainter as she slipped back into oblivion: "Why? Why? Why?"

◊

She regained consciousness in a cozy living room with blond-oak walls and a picture window overlooking the sea. A middle-aged woman offered her tea. "It's chamomile with lots of honey in it. Do you want anything to eat?"

"No. No thanks." Samantha strained to talk further, but her tongue refused to respond. The room turned fuzzy. Nausea welled up in her throat, then subsided. And as hard as she tried, she couldn't stay awake.

◊

Samantha emerged from a dark tunnel in her mind, and willed her eyes to open. She scowled at the brightness of the room. *How did I get to Mom and Dad's house?*

Her head throbbed. The refreshing aroma of mint tea floated from the kitchen.

Involuntary recollections flashed into her mind. Green mint leaves. Teal-green waves. Yellow-green eyes filled with tears. She sobbed.

A familiar voice spoke. "Samantha?" Sweet almond aftershave —

"Dad?" His hair, normally brown, now had grey at the temples. His face hid behind an unfamiliar vista of wrinkles and valleys. She peered closer. Squinted. *Yes. It's really him.*

He grinned with the playful expression that always made her feel safe, and he poked her nose. "You're back again."

"What happened? You look older. Did you find Jamie? How did I get here?"

Mr. Fischer's response seemed tentative, uneasy. "Jamie's boat was wrecked." His chin quivered. "They never found him. All they recovered was a single lifejacket. Someone who lives near the marina discovered you two weeks ago. But you've been missing for ten years."

"Ten years?" Samantha bolted to an upright position on the sofa. She touched the necklace around her throat. *Necklace?* She tugged at it and glanced down. An emerald glistened from a starfish-setting on a soft, intricately woven cord. She stared into the gem. It grew warm in her hand. *I can't remember anything, but somehow I know this necklace is important.* "Ten years?"

"Ten years. We thought you were dead. When the police told me you'd been discovered, I figured they were mistaken, or that maybe someone was playing a cruel joke. But it was you, and you look the same as you did the day you sailed off. You're still my pretty little girl."

She stood to hug him. His outdoorsy smell reawakened images of camping trips, fishing out on the bay, and slow hikes along the shore. "Where's Mom?"

His body grew rigid. "She ..." His voice cracked. "She's gone. She had a heart attack two years ago."

Father and daughter swayed in their sadness as sounds of the rising tide swished through the open window.

She broke away. "Mom's gone? Jamie, my job, my friends, my apartment. I'll have to start all over again. Ten years?"

"Ten and a half, actually. You were taken to the hospital after they found you. The police asked you questions, but you didn't have any answers. You kept waking up and asking where you were. We told you. You forgot and went back to sleep. Then it repeated all over again. Other than that, the psychiatrist and doctors say you're okay. I insisted they let me bring you home."

She sank onto the sofa and held her head in her hands. "What happened? Why can't I remember?"

◊

Samantha's dad suggested that she stay in the guestroom until her recuperation was complete. A week later, they chatted over breakfast before he went to work.

She kissed the top of his head after pouring him a fresh cup of coffee. "I think my short-term memory is back. Living at home must have been the cure."

"You're looking better every day."

"But it's hard. Everything is so different now."

"It'll get easier, Sammie. I thought I'd lose my mind when your mother died, but you know what they say about life. It goes on. Whether we want it to or not."

"What could have happened to me?"

"Whatever it was, it must have been good. You look healthy and well-cared-for." He chuckled. "And you smile in your sleep."

"You watch me sleeping?"

"Sometimes. You're still my little girl, and I worry about you. Things will get better. Give it time."

◊

The weeks crawled by as Samantha mourned her mother and Jamie. She talked to her dad about taking refresher courses so she could return to nursing. But he insisted on waiting. "Why waste money on something you might forget?"

So while he went to work, she moped around the house, learned how to load books onto the e-reader he bought her, and browsed the internet. But she often sat in silence, staring at nothing, wondering about the elusive missing element in her life.

The emerald necklace never disappeared from her neck. It warmed under her fingertips whenever she stroked it. Glowed when she looked into its depths. It comforted her and stimulated fragmented recollections of the creature with the green eyes.

One day, Samantha strolled along the beach, splashing in wave pools and wiggling her toes in the foam. She caressed the emerald and waded into the ocean. Deep. Deeper. The water covered her shoulders.

With a shuddering gasp, she turned and waded back to shore, fixating on the seaweed washing against the rocks. *Sooner or later, I'll remember. I have to.*

As more weeks dragged on, she dreamt about the creature, waking afterward in a cold sweat. Always the same beginning, always the same end:

Rhythmic pulsations relaxed her. Repeating patterns of light flashed and sparkled: beautiful, expanding patterns. Salty seaweed scents wafted in the wind. A breathy voice called her. The creature beckoned. She drifted to it.

Whenever she woke, it took several seconds for her to reorient, to realize the dream wasn't real.

The darkness was real. The thunder of her dad's snoring in the next bedroom was real. The swish of the surf breaking against the nearby rocks was real.

An increasing number of hours consisted of walking on the beach and gazing out to the horizon. She retreated into retrospection, and struggled to ignore the worried look on her dad's face.

On an overcast morning at low tide, she tiptoed into a hollowed-out cave at the water's edge, rested against a smooth rock, and slept.

Rhythmic pulsations relaxed her. Repeating patterns of light flashed and sparkled: beautiful, expanding patterns. Salty seaweed scents wafted in the wind. A breathy voice called her. The creature beckoned. She drifted to it. It changed form and became a being with yellow-green eyes, square jaw, and warm lips.

Kai.

He apologized. "My BioInterFace Fluxxatron malfunctioned. I could not save your friend."

She didn't understand, but she nodded. His breath on her skin caused shivers of anticipation.

He whispered, "Do you trust me? Do you want me?"

She leaned back. Succumbed to the passion of his lips on her neck and breasts. She murmured, "Yes. Oh, yes."

He laid her on a bed of silky softness and undressed her. She yielded. She loved.

She woke.

Samantha's cheeks were awash with tears. She caressed the emerald. *Kai gave this to me. Kai. Oh, Kai. I don't understand.*

She plodded to the house and undressed for a shower, puzzling over her appearance in the mirror. She fluffed her hair. Admired her wrinkle-free complexion. *Ten years?* Her gaze strayed to her stomach. *There. Why didn't I notice them before?*

Almost-invisible stretch marks.

She gasped.

How could she tell her dad? He wouldn't understand. He'd tell her she was imagining things.

◊

Samantha returned to the cave several times, but always woke after Kai made love to her. Her preoccupation intensified. The desire to know more filled every waking moment, every sleeping moment … until the afternoon she borrowed her dad's boat and navigated to where Jamie's craft had gone down. She turned off the engine and allowed the boat to drift while she listened to the seagulls.

She leaned back against a lifejacket and let the cries of the birds lull her into a floating reverie: "Kai. Kai. Kai."

Her whispering lips replied, "Kai." And she slept.

Kai held a baby. Their baby. Suddenly, he was an eight-year-old boy with a serious expression and green eyes like his daddy. Samantha remembered him. Loved him. She reached …

And woke.

Samantha sobbed into the depths. "Are you there?" She wept into the sky. "Are you there?" She wailed, "Kai! Analu!"

The only response was the slapping of waves against the hull.

She peered into the deep azure sea and leaned far forward over the railing. For a fleeting moment, the thought of slipping into the water enticed her. However, she forced herself back and started the engine. *I've got to tell Dad he's a grandfather.*

But she couldn't.

Every day she sailed to the same spot, dreamt the same dream, and wept. *I want to be with my husband and child. But how?*

On the tenth day, she grasped the emerald and held it to her heart. She folded both palms over it and murmured, "Kai, Analu," as she fell asleep.

Kai whispered, "You must choose your path. Your world or our world. Your people or our people. Once you choose, you can never go back. We love you, but the choice must be yours."

◊

Samantha's father scrutinized her during supper. Her preoccupied silence had become commonplace, but tonight her mood was even quieter than usual. "What's the matter, Sammie?"

"Could you take me to the exact place where they found me?"

"Sure. It's a few hundred yards down the beach. Do you remember something?"

"I think so. I need to go there before I tell you though."

They walked into the wind, and she grabbed his hand. "I love you, Dad."

He grinned. "I love you too. I'm always here for you, Sammie."

They dodged incoming breakers, laughing as the foamy waves filled their shoes with sand and salty water.

He slowed his pace. "See the rock over there that looks like it came from Stonehenge? And the dock? You were here, between them."

Samantha clutched the emerald, looked at her feet, and gazed into the green eyes of a sable Burmese cat.

◊

"Sammie?" Dad's voice. So far away. "Sammie!"

Sunlight and surf and sand. The cat sat on one side of her, and her dad knelt on the other. She rose to her knees and scratched the cat behind the ears.

It purred.

She hugged her father. "Dad, suppose you were a grandpa, but you might never be able to see your grandson. Would you still want to know?"

"Of course, Sammie, and I'd move planet and stars to see the boy." He held her at arm's length. Studied her face.

She pulled up her shirt and hitched down her shorts a few inches. "You're a grandpa." She endeavored to explain, but his confused expression stabbed at her heart.

He steepled his fingers under his nose. "Let me take you home, Sammie. You've had a hard day. We can talk about this in the morning."

She picked up the cat and kissed its nose. "Soon."

◊

Breakfast. Small talk. No mention of the previous day.

Samantha's father frowned at her with an appraising eye. "Are you sure you'll be all right by yourself? I can ask someone to come and stay with you for a few hours."

She poked his belly. "I'm okay. Let's talk about something else — like your paunch. You've been eating too much. Time for a diet, starting tonight." She hugged him. "I love you, Dad. You mean the world to me."

He poked her nose. "The paunch is *your* fault. Too much good cooking."

Another hug. "I love you so much. You have a good day at work and don't worry about li'l ol' me. Go. Now."

"Fine. I'll clear out so you can dance on the ceiling or whatever it is you do when I leave." He winked, and walked down the hallway. The back door closed behind him with a gentle click.

Samantha groaned. *He'd have me committed if he knew what I plan to do. Where's that pad of paper he uses for his doodles? There ... Now what do I say?*

She spent more than an hour writing, wadding pieces of paper into scrunched balls that landed in the wastebasket, and rewriting. *That's as good as it's going to get.*

◊

The cat was waiting for her at the spot near the strange stone on the beach. Samantha picked him up and stepped into the pounding surf. The cat purred as the water grew deeper. An undulating shimmer surrounded them, and they disappeared.

◊

When Mr. Fischer returned home from work, he discovered Samantha's note on the kitchen table. His shoulders sagged lower with every paragraph of her parting words. He sobbed. "Sammie. My poor, poor, Sammie."

He trudged into the living room and entreated her photo above the fireplace, "What do I have left to live for? Your mother is gone. Now, you're gone too."

He scuffed his feet on the carpet. Paced. Threw his head back. Looked out the window at the waves breaking against the shore. "Yes, I believe you, sweetie."

Mr. Fischer walked to the place where Samantha had been found, and he waded into the water, whispering her name into the wind.

◊

Friends found the note in the kitchen, but they never found the bodies.

Locals claim they can still hear the seagulls cry: "Kai. Kai. Kai." And the surf whispering its reply: "Sammie. Sammie. Sammie."

AFTERWORD

I'd like to talk to you about reviews.

Positive comments and ratings help authors earn a living. I urge you to post a review at your favorite online bookstore. If you didn't like what you read, please get in touch and tell me why. I'll try to address your concerns:

Author@KathySteinemann.com

And remember Joseph Addison's observation: "Reading is to the mind what exercise is to the body."

Keep reading.

Kathy

ABOUT THE EDITOR

Kathy Steinemann — Grandma Birdie to her grandkids — lives near the Rocky Mountains in the land of Atwood and Shatner and Bieber. She loves words, especially when those words are frightening or futuristic or funny.

As a young child, she scribbled poems and stories. During the progression of her love affair with words, she won public-speaking and writing awards, and she contributed to her school newspaper.

Her career has taken varying directions, including positions as editor of a small-town newspaper, computer-network administrator, and webmaster. She has also worked on projects in commercial art and cartooning.

She writes in various genres, including humor, science fiction, and historical fiction. On her website, KathySteinemann.com, she also provides free resources for writers.

Kathy loves to interact with her readers, and welcomes feedback and questions.

BOOKS BY KATHY STEINEMANN

Humor
- *Nag Nag Nag: Megan and Emmett Volume I*
- *Rule 1: Megan and Emmett Volume II*

Speculative Fiction/Multiple Genre
- *Envision: Future Fiction*
- *Suppose: Drabbles, Flash Fiction, and Short Stories*

Alternative History
- *Vanguard of Hope: Sapphire Brigade Book 1*
- *The Doctor's Deceit: Sapphire Brigade Book 2*

Nonfiction
- *The Writer's Lexicon: Descriptions, Overused Words, and Taboos*
- *The Writer's Lexicon Volume II: More Descriptions, Overused Words, and Taboos*
- *The Writer's Body Lexicon: Body Parts, Actions, and Expressions*
- *IBS-IBD Fiber Charts: Soluble & Insoluble Fibre Data for Over 450 Items, Including Links to Internet Resources*
- *The IBS Compass: Irritable Bowel Syndrome Tips, Information, Fiber Charts, and Recipes*
- *Top Tips for Packing Your Suitcase: Tips, Hints, and Advice: How, Why, and What to Pack for Your Next Travel Adventure*
- *Top Tips for Travel by Air: Over 300 Targeted Travel Tips*

Multilingual
- *Life, Death and Consequences: A selection of dual-language German-English short stories and poetry*
- *Leben, Tod und Konsequenzen: Eine Auswahl zweisprachiger Kurzgeschichten und Gedichte in Deutsch und Englisch*
- *Matthew and the Pesky Ants: Dual-language English-German short stories and poetry*
- *Matthias und die verflixten Ameisen: Zweisprachige Kurzgeschichten und Gedichte in Deutsch und Englisch*

www.ingramcontent.com/pod-product-compliance
Lightning Source LLC
Chambersburg PA
CBHW071913220626
47052CB00002B/338